A Nun's G

A novel set in the Vale Royal of England

Alan K Leicester

Illustrated by Patricia Kelsall

**An imprint of
ANNE LOADER
PUBLICATIONS**

ISBN
1 901253 08 2

Published July 1998
Reprinted February 1999

Published by:
Léonie Press
an imprint of
Anne Loader Publications
13 Vale Road
Hartford
Northwich
Cheshire CW8 1PL
Gt Britain
01606 75660

Printed by:
Anne Loader Publications

Contents

Alan K Leicester

About the author

Alan K Leicester was born in Northwich in 1941 and has lived and worked all his life in the area. He is a family man and grandfather and is now semi-retired.

For years he has enjoyed writing short poems and anecdotes, mostly of a humorous nature, for friends and colleagues, but he has always harboured a desire to produce something more serious. "A Nun's Grave" is the fulfilment of that desire.

It is his first and, he says, maybe his only, novel and reflects some of his experiences in the beautiful Cheshire countryside, in particular the area around Vale Royal Abbey and the River Weaver where he indulges in his favourite pastime of angling.

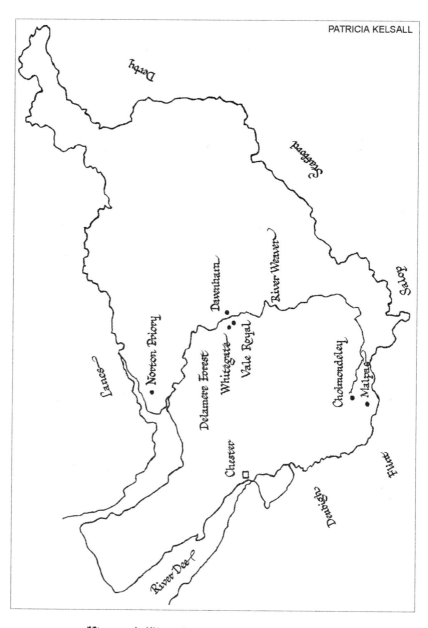

PATRICIA KELSALL

Map of Cheshire in medieval times

iv

Preface

Near to the village of Whitegate, in Cheshire, stands a rambling, red sandstone building on the site where, during the thirteenth and fourteenth centuries, stood the great Abbey of Vale Royal. This abbey, founded in 1277 by King Edward the First, was at its time the largest and finest Cistercian abbey church in the country.

Sadly, the Abbey has long since disappeared, but its legacy to the surrounding countryside and villages manifests itself in street names such as Abbey Way and Abbotsway, a nearby lake, Nunsmere, and a public house, the Vale Royal Abbey Arms: names which have survived the passage of time, though the original Abbey has itself been gone these 400 years and more.

The current building, the Manor House, has had a variety of uses over the years, latterly as offices, and work is currently under way on the site on the development of luxury housing and a golf course complex.

Within the former abbey grounds, and only a few yards from the existing building stood, for many years, a large stone monument known locally as "The Nun's Grave", bearing an inscription which read: "IDA MARIAN GODMAN, Ye Nun of St. Mary's Convent, Cestr."

Why, I wondered, had a nun been buried some eighteen miles away from her convent, within the boundaries of what had been an exclusively male and strictly celibate establishment?

This was a question which had perplexed me since, as a young man, I had fished the nearby River Weaver.

In the following pages, in a mixture of historical facts and imagination, together with the manipulation of a few dates and their historical sequence, I offer my explanation. I must stress however that it is a work of fiction and that although the locations exist the characters – and what happens to them – are my own invention.

Alan Leicester
Spring 1998

A little rule, a little sway,
A sunbeam in a winter's day,
Is all the proud and mighty have
Between the cradle and the grave.
John Dyer (1699-1757)

Chapter One

It was my third "last cast" of the day, a glorious, warm July day in 1963. The orange-tipped float drifted slowly down with the current, checking, lifting, as I controlled the release of line from the reel, then running on downstream to the spot where the shoal of fish had gathered to feed. Another yard, and it dipped sharply beneath the surface. I struck smoothly and felt the satisfying thump through the rod as the hook was driven home. A brief tussle ensued but, a few moments later, another lovely, plump Weaver roach was gently, lovingly almost, slipped into my keep-net.

Reluctantly, I decided that it was time to call it a day. Despite the warmth of the afternoon, as evening had drawn on and the sun fallen behind the trees, a damp chill had started to develop and besides, I thought, if I didn't go now it would be too late to call for a pint or two at my local pub, the perfect end to a perfect day.

Ten minutes later, my tackle packed away, I trudged contentedly in the gathering gloom along the river bank past the disused sewerage-bed for the old Manor House, towards the stile leading on to the drive.

Reaching the stile I glanced towards my van, a battered old Austin A35, and saw, in the half-light of dusk, a shadowy figure in a long grey hooded coat, standing near the rear door, peering in through the rear window. As I climbed the stile, my rod-bag snagged on something and it took me a second or two to free it. Stepping down, I glanced again towards the van. The figure had vanished.

A cold shiver ran through me as I approached the vehicle, and the hair on my neck seemed to crawl. There was nowhere that the figure could have gone in so short a time, yet there was now no sign of it. I threw my tackle into the back of the van and scrambled into the driving seat, determined to get away as fast as possible. A dreadful sensation that I was being watched came over me, and an even more awful feeling that the van was not going to start. It did, thank God, and I revved the engine fiercely, the noise reassuring and comforting!

As I moved away, the feeling of being watched became more intense, and I sensed another presence in the van. I was convinced that whoever, or whatever, it was I had seen, had somehow got into the vehicle and was, even now, sitting in the back seat. The urge to look in the mirror was tremendous, but the absolute terror of what I feared I might see was even stronger.

I rattled along the drive as fast as I dared go, and much faster than I safely should, ignoring the pot-holes and scraping branches, through the dark arched vaults of trees, the van bouncing and swaying, unreasoning fear urging me on, desperate to reach the main road before whatever it was could possess me.

Almost crying with fear and relief, I reached the junction with the Northwich by-pass near to Hartford Bridge and still I dared not look in the mirror. One thing I was sure of, my tackle would be staying in the van overnight, for nothing would make me open that back door again before daylight.

And so it was to be. Arriving home, I locked the van, practically ran into the house, stripped off, and ran a hot bath. Afterwards I dressed quickly and headed for the pub, determined to bolster my shattered nerves with a pint or two.

In the bar of the "Oddies" my fears began to dissolve in direct response to my intake of bitter and I soon felt comfortable enough to recount a part of my experience to old Bert, sitting in his customary corner near the door, though not, of course, how scared I had been.

Bert sipped his beer and nodded, smiling an odd little smile. The others within earshot laughed and suggested I had already had too much to drink, that I was making it all up. As I recounted my tale a picture of the strange figure came back into my mind. Suddenly the cold shiver came back, and with it an awful feeling, one of despair and loneliness. Better get another pint, I thought, or a drop of whisky; must have caught a chill, stayed too late near that damned river. Damned? What was I talking about? I loved the place.

Moving back to where old Bert sat, I grinned sheepishly, and decided to let the subject drop. Old Bert, however, had different ideas.

"The Nun's Grave, lad, the Nun's Grave," he whispered to me. "They don't believe you, but I do. She's said to walk sometimes, is Ida, maybe today's one of those times."

I didn't know it then, but it seemed that I'd just met Ida...

Chapter Two

asteurella pestis, bubonic plague, the Black Death, swept through Asia and Europe during the fourteenth century, killing over fifty million people.

The tiny village of Cholmondeley, in Cheshire, like so many villages on the English side of the border with Wales, was built in the shelter of a castle which offered protection against the marauding bands of thieves and outlaws who would periodically sweep down from the Welsh hills, pillaging, stealing cattle and sheep, and generally terrorising the populace.

As a defence against this greater and more malignant foreign invader, the Black Death, the castle had proved utterly useless. Of a population of over one hundred souls, barely a score had survived. Just a few weeks before the little village green had rung to the sounds of laughter as the band of travelling players had passed through. They had brought to the village a glimpse of the outside world rarely seen by these simple folk, together with tales of strange lands over the sea, and the great cities they had visited, the sights they had seen.

They had also brought the plague.

Within a week of their leaving, the deaths had started. Whole families were wiped out in days – young and old, frail babies, strong young farmhands – the disease showed no favours and death took most of those it touched.

Among those few so far spared were the old village priest, Father Mayman, and an old woman and her daughter, the Godmans. Their cottage was just outside the village, in a clearing on the edge of a little wood. The old lady was greatly revered, feared even, by the simple villagers. She was believed to be a witch, though none dared mouth the word in her presence. As a consequence the girl, Ida, was a lonely child, largely spurned by the rest of the village children, her closest friend the great black cat which was her constant companion.

This unlikely combination of old and young, innocent and

4

ungodly, had worked together trying to stem the tide of deaths, but neither the prayers of the priest nor the potions of the "witch" could hold the disease in check.

There was no time now to bury the corpses, so numerous were they, and they were being burned each day on a great funeral pyre on the village green. How long they could continue to do this the priest did not know. Soon there would not be enough fit persons left alive to cut and carry the fuel needed for this grim task. When a whole family was found dead together, it was simpler to torch the cottage, and this was being done, the primitive huts with their thatched roofs burning fiercely, consuming the occupants and the parasites which carried the dreadful disease.

The stench of death hung over the village and the old priest wept with despair at his helplessness. Then old Mother Godman was taken. As Father Mayman approached the cottage Ida stepped out of the door, the cat, as ever, rubbing round her legs.

"My mother is dying," she said, dry-eyed and seemingly without emotion. "She is asking for you."

Entering the tiny cottage the priest found the old woman on a little cot in a corner of the room. One glance told him that what the girl had said was true, the woman was indeed dying: he had seen far too many die to hold out any false hopes that she might be spared. He knelt at the side of the cot and reached out his hand to administer the last rites. Her hand clutched his with surprising strength, pushing it away from her face, as she said:

"I am not of your faith, priest, save your blessings for those who believe. I ask only one favour of you, that you care for the girl, she has no-one here now and she will need a friend."

She pressed a scrap of parchment into the priest's hand.

"I have a sister in Chester, this is her address, if the girl can reach her I know she will help."

Father Mayman nodded: "If it is God's will to spare me I will see that the child reaches her aunt, this I swear. Now rest, I will send Ida to you."

He left the cottage and found the girl sitting on a stool by the door, the huge black cat stretched across her lap. Few cats now

5

existed in the village, but of this one the villagers had a latent fear, belonging as it did to the "witch's" daughter.

They were a superstitious lot and many believed there was a direct link between the devil and the disease, and all knew that cats, particularly black cats, were the devil's messengers. Cats had been drowned and burnt to death, but still the plague raged through the land. Had they known the truth of the matter, that the disease was carried by the fleas on rats, they would have realised that those same cats, rather than being their enemies, might well have proved to be their greatest allies in their fight for life. But, with ignorance had come fear, a fear not foreign to the priest, testing even his faith in the Almighty.

"Go to your mother, child, she needs you now," he said gently, reaching out to touch her head.

At his sudden movement the cat hissed and spat, needle-sharp fangs bared and a great hooked claw stretched out in defence of the girl. She whispered something in its ear and rose from the stool, dropping the animal to the ground. The cat ran into the cottage and the girl followed, a strange smile on her face.

Through the night Ida nursed her mother, giving what comfort she could as she watched the deadly disease take its inexorable toll, but just before the dawn, during one of the bouts of delirium symptomatic of the plague, a great shuddering spasm seized the old woman and life passed from her.

For a few minutes the girl sat at the cot-side, gazing into the tortured face, then, without a sound and without tears, covered it with the ragged blanket. They had been inseparable for all of Ida's sixteen years, with little contact with the other villagers, yet the girl showed no great emotion, no great sense of loss. Her mother had been greatly feared in the village, though people would come to her, in times of sickness, for the medicines she concocted from herbs and other plants.

Ida had watched and listened as her mother produced these potions and balms, and was familiar with many of the plants used. On the shelves near the fireplace were numerous pots and packets which Ida knew contained the ingredients of many of the

6

cures her mother had sold to the villagers. Already the girl's mind was beginning to plan for the future. She had never known her father, and her mother had never spoken of him. To Ida it was of no great import, her mother, and in recent years the cat, had been company enough. The cat had just arrived one day, and taken up residence with them, as if it were the most natural thing in the world. Neither had thought it strange, though to the villagers it was further evidence of their link with the devil and his ways.

Ida began to place the packages and jars on her bed, subconsciously readying herself to move away from this place where she had lived all her life, though not knowing where she would go. She knew that she had only been tolerated in the village because of the fear her mother engendered among the superstitious villagers. Now the old woman was gone it would not take long for the surviving villagers to vent their spleen on her. It was time to go.

As daylight came Father Mayman appeared at the door. He stooped and peered in, seeing the untidy heap on the bed and realising that the old woman had died.

He turned to Ida. "God bless you, my child," he murmured softly. "She asked me to care for you. She spoke of an aunt in Chester and we must make arrangements to get you to her as soon as possible."

Chester lay over twelve miles to the west of the village, and, in normal times, pack trains passed through on a regular basis, taking people, livestock and goods to the markets and fairs. Since the coming of the plague none had been seen and the priest realised he would have to think of something else. Before that, however, there were other things to do. Another person had died during the night and there was the cremation to attend to.

To Ida he said: "I shall return shortly with some help. We will attend to your mother, then you must come to stay with me until we can get you to your aunt."

The girl nodded but made no reply, and the old man went about his business.

When he returned an hour or so later with a couple of men from the village, it was to find the cottage in flames and the girl stand-

7

ing some yards away, a bundle of belongings at her feet, the cat in her arms, watching the sparks and smoke rising to the sky. Still there was no trace of sorrow, no sign of grief, only an enquiring look at the priest.

"It is done," she said, "I am ready to go."

For the next three days and nights the girl stayed at the priest's house. During this period there was only one more death in the village, and Father Mayman was praying that the epidemic had peaked and that the worst might be over. Conversation between the pair was sparse. Ida seemed to have retreated into herself and any remarks to her were greeted with the briefest of replies, if at all.

Conscious of his vow to the dying woman, Father Mayman had by now decided that the only way to fulfil it would be for him to accompany Ida on the long journey. It was not a task he relished, but, having made his decision, he set about the preparations for the journey. He decided that they would start out two days later, early in the morning so that they would have a full day in which to walk the twelve miles or so to their destination. He informed the girl of his decision that evening.

She greeted this information with her usual seeming indifference and sat staring into the fire, the cat at her side, as it had been constantly since her mother's death. Something about this odd couple troubled the priest and he had a strange foreboding.

News had come in from a passing tinker that the disease had affected the entire area for miles around, so it seemed that the travellers could expect little help on their journey, other than that of the God in whom the old man so devoutly believed.

When the day of departure came they set off along the bridle-path, old priest and young girl, their bundles on their backs. Of the cat there was no sign.

Chapter Three

Two hours slow walking had brought the couple to the edge of the priest's parish, and beyond this distance he had only rarely travelled, and the girl never. Father Mayman's efforts over the last few weeks had brought him almost to the state of physical and spiritual exhaustion, and he realised that they must soon rest and take sustenance. There was only one other small farmhouse along their route whose occupants he was acquainted with. They were the Bickerton family, and he determined to leave the road at the turn-off to their property, knowing that he would be hospitably received there.

They reached the little lane that ran down to the farmhouse and turned wearily into it. As they neared the little cluster of buildings they became aware of the awful death stench which they had but a short time before left behind them in the village. A few yards more brought them into the farmyard where the source of the smell became immediately apparent.

The body of John Bickerton lay near the open doorway of the little house, a revolting cloud of flies swarming round the bloody mask which had been his face, and the blackened pool of blood in which he lay. His had not been a quick death. This much was obvious from the trail of blood, across the yard from the nearby barn, which traced his tortured attempt to reach the house.

Fearing the worst, the priest stepped over the body and into the farmhouse. As his eyes became accustomed to the gloom inside, he was able to make out another figure on the earthen floor. Anne Bickerton must have put up a good fight but the odds had obviously been too great. Her naked body was a shocking sight. Her breasts were badly bruised and bore bite marks, her stomach and thighs were covered in blood, but she was still alive, though barely so.

As the old priest leaned over her she began to whimper like a child. He laid a gentle hand on her brow and she flinched and moaned, a broken hand feebly reaching out to try to push him away.

9

"Peace, my child," he whispered, "It is Father Mayman, I will not harm you."

She seemed to understand his words but was incapable of reply. Her jaw was broken or dislocated, her lips a bloody pulp. The priest covered her with a blanket from the bed in the corner of the room and turning to Ida he said:

"Light a fire and warm some water, we will do what we can for her."

The girl seemed not to hear, her eyes never leaving the woman's body, her face a mask of horror at what she saw.

"Move, girl," the priest shouted. "Light the fire, bring the water, quickly now."

His words and the raised voice broke through Ida's state of shock and she moved to obey him.

A short time later a small fire was crackling in the hearth and a pan of water was placed on it to warm. The priest had attempted to move Anne to the bed in the meantime, but his efforts had brought shuddering moans of agony from the woman. He realised that, apart from spiritual comfort, there was going to be little he could do for her. Ida poured a little of the warm water into a cup, and into it stirred a pinch of powder from one of the packets in her bundle.

"This will take away the pain," she said, pushing past the priest.

Raising the woman's head she poured the potion into the poor, broken mouth and, though much of it spilled from her mouth down her naked breasts mingling with the blood oozing there, she managed to swallow some and, after a little while, the moaning stopped and the woman seemed to relax. Behind the girl the priest crossed himself. Even his faith did not allow him to totally disregard the stories he had heard back in the village about the magical powers of the Godmans.

Less than an hour later Anne Bickerton died. She never regained consciousness but seemed to suffer no further pain. Together, Ida and the priest carried the broken body of her husband into the house and laid it alongside hers. Father Mayman knew that there had been no children, and for this, at least, he was thankful.

With the rest of the water that Ida had warmed, they mixed a little oatmeal and after this simple meal the priest knelt briefly in prayer beside the couple.

Then, climbing wearily to his feet, he said. "We have not the strength to bury them, you and I. Make a torch, we will burn the farmhouse."

The place was tinder dry and the fire raced through it, consuming everything within minutes. As they stood and watched the priest cried out:

"May their murderers be damned, O Lord, may they burn in the flames of hell forever!"

A brief search around the farmyard revealed nothing. There was no trace of food and all the livestock had vanished, the place had been systematically looted. They turned their backs on the fire and walked away, each fearing for the future but neither wishing to confide in the other.

Leaving the farm track they turned west onto the main bridle path toward Chester. The priest reckoned that with no further delays, and allowing an hour or so for breaks, they should arrive in the city in the late afternoon.

They trudged slowly on, engrossed in their own thoughts. The priest was in agonies of doubt. Why did his God allow such evil in the world? His faith was being tested as never before and, for the first time in his life, doubts were beginning to creep into his mind. Never before had God failed him, but the dreadful events of the past weeks, and the horrific scenes back at the Bickerton house, had him asking why He should allow such evil to triumph.

Ida, on the other hand, had no such doubts. Her life had always been one of hardship, her gods were the gods of the woods, fields and streams, the animals and birds, her religion a much more ancient one than the priest's. She had heard her mother talk to these gods, asking for their help, offering sacrifices to them, appeasing, bargaining for power. She had wandered alone for hours through the woods and meadows, seeking out the plants her mother worked with, those such as camomile and borage, used in healing potions and salves, and others like hemlock and deadly nightshade, with other, more nefarious properties.

She had watched and learned as these were ground or boiled to produce the pastes and potions she now carried in the bundle on her shoulder. She was aware of the power this knowledge could give her and aware, also, of the potential danger that same power could bring if used unwisely.

To Ida life had so far been very simple. Take what nature made available and use it to your best advantage: that had been her mother's teaching and it was her intent to continue to live by that creed.

Eventually they came within sight of a little hamlet, just a few thatched cottages huddled together, as if for shelter, at the edge of a small coppice. Though there was no sign of life, a drift of woodsmoke amongst the buildings seemed to indicate that one, at least, was occupied.

Mindful of the possible danger, Father Mayman decided to go on alone, leaving his pack with Ida, hidden at the edge of the copse.

"You will stay here until I shout that it is safe to come out," he told the girl, "we must take no chances. You have seen what animals men can become, stay hidden until I call."

So saying, the old man walked slowly on into the little village. Ida watched from the bushes as he approached the first of the dwellings, saw him enter and re-emerge. She watched as four men appeared from the next house, watched as they surrounded the priest, saw them begin to taunt him, heard their drunken voices as they danced around him. She heard his voice raised in protest at this treatment of the cloth, heard again the drink in the voices of his tormentors, then watched as they began to systematically beat him, first with their fists and feet, and then with wooden staves, until he could take no more and fell to the ground. She watched too, as they brought a length of rope from the house, one end of which they tied round the old man's neck. The other they threw over the branch of a nearby tree. They stripped the old man of his clothing and she looked on in horrified silence as the four of them hauled on the rope and dragged the old man clear of the ground, his feet kicking and his hands hopelessly clutching at the rope, trying to loosen the noose which was choking the life out of him. They tied the rope off round the trunk of the tree and again commenced to beat the old priest with the long staves. When all signs of life had left the hanging, naked figure they tired of their gruesome sport and, laughing again, staggered back into the house from which they had come.

Ida remained in her hiding-place for a long time. Not until complete silence had settled over the place did she attempt to move. She then crept slowly down towards the buildings, stopping every few yards to listen and watch, until she was almost at the house which held the killers. She could now see the blackened face of the priest, tongue protruding, sightless eyes staring, as the bruised and bloodied body spun slowly round on the rope, the ground beneath him stained by the contents of his bladder and bowels, involuntarily evacuated in the poor man's death throes. She felt no great sorrow at his death, no great loss, but, nonetheless, a sense that this had been a good man who had not deserved to die in such a manner. A surge of anger flared up in her at his treatment. She knew that he had died helping her, and therefore it was her duty to repay him for his sacrifice.

Moving to the partially open door of the house she paused again to listen. The only sounds she could hear were of drunken snoring. Slowly she pushed open the door. The stench from the room was appalling. She stepped carefully into the single room and took in the scene. The four men lay on the straw-covered floor, smeared in their own filth like the animals they were, in a drunken stupor.

Her eyes moved around the single room, assessing the situation. A single oil lamp cast its flickering yellow light over the tiny room. A few logs smouldered in the open hearth, the smoke from them adding to the fug and stinging her eyes. Next to the hearth was a heap of kindling and dried rushes and close by, a large earthenware jug. She moved slowly to the fireside and picked up the jug. It was warm from the fire and contained, as she had expected, a mixture of oil and fat to be used for cooking purposes, and as fuel for the rush lamps.

Approaching one of the sleeping killers she carefully poured a quantity of the oil around his back and shoulders and into the straw on which he lay. She froze as he groaned and shifted, but he did not wake and she moved around the room, anointing each figure as she went. Gathering up a handful of straw from the floor she twisted it to form a torch, which she dipped into the jug. What oil remained she then poured over the bundles of rushes which she carefully positioned between the still sleeping brutes and the cottage door. Finally, she thrust the torch into the fire where it burst into flames, then dragged it back across the floor to the doorway, igniting the kindling and straw as she went.

Picking up one of the heavy staves with which the men had beaten the old priest, she took up a position a couple of yards from the doorway and waited. The draught through the open door fanned the flames and, within minutes, the building was ablaze, parts of the roof thatch beginning to fall inside to add further fuel to the inferno.

Whether it was the smoke that killed the others Ida did not know, but, of the four killers, only one managed to make it as far as the doorway in an attempt to escape. As he began to emerge the end of Ida's stave thudded viciously into his chest. There was a loud crack as his breastbone shattered and he was propelled, screaming, back into the flames. She stepped back as the heat became more fierce, then stood motionless, the flames reflected in dark unfeeling eyes, until the screaming stopped and the execution was completed. The priest's words echoed through her head:

"May they burn in the flames of hell forever."

"Amen to that, priest," she murmured, and turned away.

She cut down the body of the priest and laid it out on the ground, hands crossed across the chest as she had seen him do to others.

"There is no more I can do, old man," she said. "May you go to your heaven, and may your God reward you."

She picked up her bundle of belongings, adding to it the few things she thought might be useful from that of the priest.

Discarding the rest she walked away, a grim smile on her face.

Reaching the spot where she had previously hidden, she drew a rough blanket from her pack and settled down for the rest of the night. Her sleep was deep and untroubled, and she awoke as day dawned, refreshed for her journey.

Now alone, her only thought was to carry on as planned and try to reach Chester, and to this purpose she strode out resolutely, the happenings of the last few hours, for the time being, pushed to the back of her partly dazed mind.

The remainder of her journey went without incident. She saw few people. The plague had not only killed people, it had taken from the survivors the desire to communicate. Fear had created isolation, but isolation was something Ida could live with, something she had grown very much accustomed to in her childhood days.

She walked for only short distances, with frequent stops between. At each dwelling or hamlet she came across she waited and watched before proceeding, mindful all the time of the dangers which could await her.

Consequently, though her journey was not great in terms of distance, on this short winter day the light was again fading as the great city walls came into view. Despite the frequent rests the girl was very tired as she reached the great arched gateway leading into the city.

It was an ancient city, its great walls and towers built originally by the Romans many centuries before, and added to over the years, as a defence against the fierce bands of Welsh marauders, still largely unsubdued, raiding with impunity the villages and towns along the border.

Under normal circumstances the gate would have been manned by sentries, but these were far from being normal times and Ida was able to pass, unchallenged, through the archway and into the dark narrow streets beyond. Even inside the city few people were abroad, and Ida wandered aimlessly for a while, not knowing how to go about finding her aunt. Among the items she had removed from the priest's pouch had been the parchment with the address on and, though she could not read, she knew that it said Watergate Street.

The light was fading quickly now and, as it did, the number of people on the streets was becoming fewer. She realised that she must now ask someone for guidance to her destination. A few more yards brought her to the entrance to an alley, now in almost complete darkness.

What at first appeared to be a pile of rags, heaped against a wall, stirred as she approached, a filthy face emerging from amongst them. She stopped and the face became a head and shoulders, as a youth of twelve or so came to his feet. Life in the city had become even harder than normal with the coming of the plague, and pickings for the footpads and pickpockets had become very scarce. This one now saw his chance to rectify that situation. A girl, little older than himself and alone on the streets after dark, would be easy to overcome and rob. She carried a goodly sized pack, and he intended to relieve her of it.

"Are you lost, girl?" he asked, sidling towards Ida. "Can I help you with your pack?"

He reached out to take it from her, but was repelled by a violent shove which sent him back against the wall.

"I only mean to help," he said. "Let me help you – tell me what you want."

Ida stared into his eyes and he knew that tonight there would be no easy pickings, not from this one. He changed his approach, sliding down the wall till he again appeared like the bundle of rags she had first seen, squatting subserviently at her feet.

Ida placed her pack on the ground, taking from it the scrap of parchment with the address, and a small leather purse containing a few copper coins. One of these she held out to the boy.

"Take me to the Watergate, and this shall be yours," she said. "Try to trick me and you will be sorry!"

The boy rose slowly to his feet. She was only a girl, no bigger than him, but something in her eyes, and the tone of her voice, worried and warned him.

"Follow me, then," he said, reaching for the coin.

She snatched it back.

"When we get there," she replied, "and no tricks, remember."

Though quite a large city it was very compact, confined as it was by the ancient walls. Ida had entered by the Eastgate, and the Watergate stood less than a quarter of a mile away, to the west of the city, facing the waters of the River Dee from which it had taken its title.

It took only a few minutes to reach Watergate Street, the address she had for her aunt, and less than that, on arrival, to realise that her journey had been pointless. The whole street had been wasted by the plague. The houses showed no signs of occupancy, no lights shone, doors and windows hung from broken hinges, many of them smashed, and a jumble of broken furniture, pottery and the like gave clear indication that the looters had been at their despicable work.

Ida stared in dismay at the mess, at a loss as to what to do next, and in that instant, while her guard was down, the lad snatched the purse from her hand and, in a flash, had vanished into the maze of alleys, his mocking laughter echoing back to her as he ran.

In that moment all the trauma of the last few hours and the fatigue of the weeks prior seemed to drain Ida of all her energy, and, for a moment or two, she was close to collapse. She staggered to the wall of a building and slid slowly down to the ground, becoming, herself, another heap of rags, indistinguishable from those others she had earlier seen. For several minutes she lay there, her mind a blank, her legs numb, her whole body crying out for rest.

Slowly she sank into a kind of stupor, the pictures in her mind tumbling round and round, the face of her dead mother, the poor abused body of the woman Anne, the bulging eyes and gaping mouth of the naked priest, the flames...

She awoke to a gentle shaking and a voice, full of compassion, asking: "Can you hear me, child? Are you hurt?"

Opening her eyes, she saw a kindly old face peering anxiously down at her. As consciousness returned she realised that the

17

speaker was a nun, and a sense of relief that there was no danger overwhelmed her. Through all the pain and torment of the past weeks she had remained dry-eyed, seemingly empty of emotion, but now, at those few kind words, she wept.

"Come, my dear," said the old nun. "I am Sister Catherine and our house is only a short walk from here. Soon you will be safe and warm. Come, let me help you."

So saying, she helped Ida to her feet and, gathering up her meagre belongings, led her gently away towards the convent and safety.

As midnight approached, in a nearby alley, Ida's young assailant lay asleep. The money he had stolen from her had bought him a good measure of strong ale and a hot meal, and now he slept, his breathing heavy, his senses dulled.

From the shadows appeared a huge black cat, yellow eyes gleaming in the meagre light. It slowly circled the sleeping lad, then climbed onto his chest and stretched out across his face, its thick fur covering his nose and mouth, its claws sinking into his ragged clothing. A few minutes later the boy's breathing had stopped.

The cat rose, stretched, then padded slowly away, vanishing into the shadows.

Chapter Four

As Jane had walked down the aisle towards him that morning, Alan Barker had turned slightly to watch her. Again he had marvelled at his luck, that all his dreams were now to come true. Jane had been his childhood sweetheart, his first and only girlfriend, and that morning she had become his wife. The ceremony had been a lovely one and all the more meaningful to them because their relationship had not included a "trial" marriage.

They had pledged to save themselves for each other, and, now that the waiting was over, they were sure that their love would be all the sweeter for it. All the usual speeches and rigmarole of the reception were behind them, and now, as he lay on the huge bed in the honeymoon suite, his thoughts were only of her.

She emerged from the bathroom where she had been for the last quarter of an hour and walked slowly towards him. She was wearing a lovely pale blue diaphanous nightdress, through which he could see her ripe young body, and the sight of her firm breasts and the dark triangle at the base of her belly were enough to arouse him immediately. She stood at the foot of the bed gazing down at him, at the huge erection now so painfully obvious, then, slipping the nightdress from her shoulders, climbed onto the bed and astride him, all in one movement.

She rode him, slowly for a few moments, then faster and faster as he began to buck beneath her, his back arching and his thighs thrusting upwards, lifting her from the bed.

In seconds it was over, a great gushing climax to the years they had waited, an outpouring of all the love they felt for each other. Ian sank back onto the bed and she lay above him, still holding him within her. Jane leaned forward, her breasts teasing his lips, her tongue playing around his ears, her hands caressing his neck and shoulders, until she felt him harden again inside her. Again she began to ride, slowly, but this time, as the tempo quickened, she rolled on to her side and then her back, her legs going round Ian's waist, her fingers digging into his back, pulling him into her with all the strength in her body. This time their climax took longer to arrive, but it was just as thrilling and somehow even more fulfilling than the first time.

They rolled apart and lay, holding hands, side by side, man and wife, together for the first time in the love act. After a few moments Jane thought that it would be nice to try a third time for further comparison, but, on turning to Ian to make her suggestion, found him to be fast asleep.

She lay for a long time studying the handsome face and the beautiful body of the man she had that day married, then tiredness overcame her and, cuddling up to her man, she, too, drifted into a dreamless sleep.

She awoke before Ian the next morning, slipped from the bed and into the bathroom to run a bath. The hotel provided lovely scented bath oils and foam and a few minutes later she sank into the water and lay back, luxuriating in the warmth as it eased the ache in her thighs and stomach. She had not realised how exhausting love-making could be; perhaps things would improve with practice, she mused.

No sooner had the thought entered her mind than her new husband entered the bathroom, and in seconds was in the bath with her. He soaped and sponged her body and she his, each paying particular attention to those parts they found most attractive, until their cleanest and most laundered parts could bear to be apart no longer.

Afterwards they laughed together, and changing the bath-water, completed their toilet with only minor interruptions. This, the second day of their honeymoon, was also to be the last. The decision had been made before they married, that whatever money they could spare would go towards the ridiculously expensive, but wonderful house they had bought.

They had both lived in Chester all their lives and had never really intended to live anywhere else, although Ian's daily journey to his job in Manchester was becoming increasingly irksome. It was while driving home one evening that he had seen the signs advertising the new housing development at Vale Royal, near the town of Northwich and eighteen miles closer to his workplace. That weekend they had driven out to the site.

For Jane it had been instant enchantment. While the houses themselves were similar to those on a dozen other sites they had visited, the environment was breathtakingly, beautifully different. The front of each house faced out onto the newly opened golf course, yet they were far enough away to maintain their privacy from all but the very worst of golfers.

At the rear, each had a long landscaped garden, sweeping down to a splendid wood, threaded with pathways, leading to the River Weaver beyond. They had only briefly explored the wooded area, but had seen enough to convince them of the beauty of the place. Great swathes of pink and purple rhododendrons stood out vividly against their dark green backcloth of polished leaves, and wild flowers bloomed in abundance wherever they looked. The woods and riverbanks teemed with wildlife – rabbits, grey squirrels, and birds of every description whose songs combined to make a chorus the like of which neither of them had previously heard.

Thus it was that later that morning, as they packed their cases and loaded them into the car, there were no regrets over the brevity of the honeymoon. On the contrary, they were now anxious to get to their new home where they would have another ten days before they were due to return to work. Another ten days to hone their new-found skills.

A couple of hours later the car turned into the driveway of their home, and, moments later, Ian carried Jane across the threshold and into the great new adventure of married life.

Of the exact nature of that adventure they were, at that time, blissfully unaware...

Chapter Five

Four months had passed since Sister Catherine had brought Ida to St. Mary's. During the first week the girl had drifted in and out of consciousness in the grip of a high fever, the trauma of the terrible events of recent weeks now exacting its toll from her young body and mind.

In her sleeping moments she was beset by vivid nightmares of funeral pyres, dead bodies, the old priest's blackened face and bulging eyes, and the flames; always there were flames, crackling, roaring, searing her skin and, above their roar, the words of the old man, "flames of hell........forever, forever, forever...."

Through all this time Sister Catherine rarely left Ida's bedside, her soft voice a constant litany, her gentle hands soothing and cooling the girl's fevered body. At last her prayers and ministrations bore fruit and Ida's ramblings gradually diminished, her sleep became less disturbed and, gradually, her health returned to normal as the fever left her.

Her illness had left her extremely weak but, little by little, as some strength returned, Ida was able to become more involved in the everyday workings of the nunnery. It was a relatively new establishment, of the Benedictine Order, and building work and recruitment were still going on. Among her earliest tasks, since it did not involve leaving the convent, was helping those survivors among the building workers as they began, once more, to take up their tasks about the place. Like everyone else they, too, had suffered as the plague had swept through the city, but now, once more, some progress was being made.

The nuns were tireless in their efforts to help those in the city most in need, and the plague ensured that there was no shortage of such needy. Hundreds had died and hundreds more had fled, panic-stricken, from the city, vainly trying to escape the invisible hand of death. For those who were stricken down the Sisters could do little; few medicines were available to cure them, and prayer was equally ineffective. Their main efforts, therefore, were directed towards helping the survivors, those mysteriously spared when all around them had died.

In the convent itself there had been deaths, three of the nuns had been taken since Ida's arrival, and there were those who believed that the events were not coincidental, and that she had brought the pestilence with her.

Ida could not, however, be criticised for her efforts to help. She was by nature a strong girl, and as her fitness returned she proved to be a tower of strength amongst the nuns, some of whom were elderly and frail, and few of whom had experienced the austere upbringing she had endured.

Each day they would leave the convent, taking such food as could be spared, and search the vermin-ridden alleys, looking for the very old and the very young, those least able to help themselves, and in this way many lives had been saved.

Ida now realised that if Sister Catherine had not found her when she did, she, too, would almost certainly have failed to survive, and she felt that she therefore owed it to the old nun to repay the debt by helping her as she worked to save others. From the powders in her pack Ida made potions and medicines, many of which were extremely effective against some of the minor ailments they encountered. She told Sister Catherine of the things she had learned at her mother's side, and the old woman watched and listened as the girl mixed her brews, marvelling at such knowledge in one so young.

As the weeks passed the epidemic began to abate. Each day fewer deaths were being reported, and those people touched by the disease who had managed to survive, seemed to suffer no recurrence of it. This seemed to be the nature of the pestilence, completely random in whom it took, whom it spared, paying no heed to age, physical condition or status. This was what made it so terrifying and seemingly inescapable, and why, even though it seemed to be receding, the good Sisters were reluctant to accept that it was over; but, as three weeks more slipped by without a death or a new outbreak, it did appear that the worst was behind them.

Life at the convent began to return to normal and the affairs of the nuns' God, which had of necessity taken a back seat over the last few months, once more came to the fore.

Sister Catherine, never far from Ida's side since she had found her, now began to question the girl about her past and her plans for the future. The girl was homeless and destitute, her mother was dead, of her aunt there was no trace, and it was reasonable to assume that she, too, had been taken by the plague.

Sister Catherine proposed to the girl that she should, under the circumstances, consider giving herself to the Church and to God. The same thought had briefly entered Ida's head recently, and been instantly rejected. Ida knew that the strict demands of the Order had, of necessity, been relaxed during the crisis which had hit the city. She also realised that the passing of the plague would signal an end to such relaxation, and that the harsh regimen of the nuns' lives would be re-established at the earliest opportunity. She had learned enough of the Order to know that her joining it would involve great personal sacrifice and hardship, the months of postulancy, the years as, initially, a novice and then a junior nun, the total dedication required was, she thought, not for her.

She had no wish to spend the rest of her life in this manner and had neither the faith nor the belief that Sister Catherine and the others held. She had, though, become very fond of the old nun, and had no desire to hurt or offend her, being, as she was, so much in her debt.

Ida also still carried her terrible secret, the death of Father Mayman's tormentors. She had told Sister Catherine much of what had happened on the journey, of the deaths of the Bickertons and Father Mayman, but of her fiery revenge she had said nothing, knowing that the old nun would not feel, as she did, that the dreadful deed was justifiable, certainly not in the eyes of God. She knew that in her mind Sister Catherine would conceive the bandits' deaths as mortal sin, whereas she considered it a natural process; ridding the world of evil was, after all, their God's aim. Ida felt no remorse, the deed was done, the evil ones were dead, no-one else need know. But could she go on living the lie, deceiv-

24

ing the old woman who had so befriended her? To this subject she must give much more thought.

Chapter Six

Today was their "anniversary": they had been married a whole month. "Who said it wouldn't last, Mr Barker?" laughed Jane as she skilfully avoided Ian's hands, which for the umpteenth time that day were trying to grab her as she passed by.

"If you want your lunch on time you'll have to behave yourself," she went on, "so make your mind up."

"I'm not keen on salad, anyway," replied Ian, "so it's no great loss, and it won't go cold either."

He had outmanoeuvred her and she was now trapped against the worktop. Ian was wearing a new shirt and Jane's hands were oily with salad dressing. For a few seconds she tried to push him away with her forearms and elbows but it was like fighting an octopus and she quickly gave up the uneven contest, and turned her attention instead to returning his caresses, and to hell with the shirt!

This was how it had been for a month. They had made love in every room in the house, every one, and at most times of the night and day, and neither of them seemed ever sated. They fed on each other's desire and thrived on each other's lust. They craved no company but each other and, to some extent, resented the occasional visitors they received.

Today they had planned a walk along the drive to the nearby village of Hartford with its shops and pubs, the homely Red Lion, near the lovely old church, and the elegant Hartford Hall, more a hotel than a pub, though equally attractive. Their weekends were precious, when work did not interfere with their being in love.

So, over the last few weekends they had developed this habit of walking, each Saturday morning, along the drive from their home into the village, a couple of miles away. It was a pleasant walk, weather permitting, through the great arches of trees which bordered the drive for most of its length.

On this particular morning they had decided that after completing their shopping they would call, on the return journey, into

Hartford Hall for a drink and a sandwich at the bar. It was a lovely old black and white building, dating back to the sixteenth century, which they had passed on several occasions, but had not, as yet, patronised, merely admiring its pleasant facade from the outside.

Arriving there, shopping completed, some two hours or so later, they found their expectations more than fulfilled. The interior of the old building contained a wealth of antique furniture, grand paintings adorned its walls and plush rugs and carpets its floors. The walls were wood panelled and at one end of the bar was a huge open-hearthed fireplace, decorated with horse brasses and a heavy brass companion set.

Settling at a table set in the window bay, opposite the bar, they ordered their drinks and food then sat back, taking in the atmosphere of the old room.

"I can just imagine this in the winter," said Jane, "with a great log fire blazing away. What a lovely room, isn't it?"

Ian nodded in agreement, but something else had taken his eye. Above a door in the corner of the room was a notice which read, "To the Nun's Suite."

At that moment the waiter arrived with their order and, after thanking him, Ian asked about the notice.

"I'm sorry, sir," the waiter replied, "I don't know the full story, but the place is reputed to be haunted – some connection with the old Abbey at Vale Royal, built on the site of one of the old estate buildings or something. Personally I think the haunting business is a load of rubbish, I've worked here for over eight years now and I've never seen or heard anything. Still, it gives the clients something to talk about."

He deposited the drinks and plates on the table and smiled,

"There are some, though, who swear there's a ghost and the boss doesn't discourage the rumours – he says it's good for business! Enjoy your meal, sir, madam."

They thanked him and he hurried away. They lingered over the sandwiches, not yet wanting to leave their opulent surroundings. Ian went to the bar to order more drinks. The barman, like the waiter, was the epitome of politeness. He was much older than the

27

waiter and had the air of an old style butler, precise and meticulous in his work.

"That will be two pounds sixty, sir," he said as he passed the drinks to Ian.

"Have one yourself," Ian replied.

"Why, thank you, sir, I'll take a half of bitter with you."

Ian returned to his seat beside Jane and nodded as the old man raised his glass to them, returning the gesture with a smile.

"What a nice old man," Jane said. "He reminds me a bit of my grand-dad."

The barman must have heard her remark and, smiling to himself, mimed a doddering walk from behind his bar to a nearby table which he proceeded to wipe with an exaggeratedly shaky hand.

Jane burst out laughing and blushed brightly, and the barman came over to their table, with the same time-worn gait, his bright eyes sparkling with mischief.

"Pardon me saying, my lady," he croaked, "but it does an old man's heart good to hear such a happy laugh from someone so young and lovely – fair made my day you have!"

Jane blushed even more and dissolved into an uncontrollable fit of giggles, while Ian and the barman laughed together at her discomfiture. When she had eventually regained her composure she explained to the barman that her remark had been intended as a compliment.

"And that's how it was taken, madam," he replied, "and thank you very much."

After that the three of them got on famously; very quickly, introductions were made and the barman, George, had become a new-found friend. More drinks were consumed and an hour or so later Ian and Jane decided that it was time to go.

As they made to leave George said to Ian, "I heard you asking young Andrew about the Nun's Suite. Take a bit of advice from your old grand-dad, Ian, don't get too involved.".

With this he turned to his washing-up and, slightly perplexed, Ian and Jane left for home.

However, as they strolled along the leafy, sunlit drive toward Vale

Royal, a little the worse for drink, his warning words were soon forgotten and their mood was one of total happiness and contentment.

Arriving home, it took only a couple of minutes to put out the sun loungers on the rear lawn and another couple for the two of them to fall asleep in the warm sunshine.

Ian awoke with a shiver.

The sun had moved round to the front of the house and was much lower in the sky. Glancing blearily at his watch he saw that it was almost eight: he had been asleep nearly four hours. Jane's chair was empty and suddenly, unreasoning blind panic overcame him. He dashed into the house calling her name, then stopped, embarrassed, as he found her at the kitchen sink, washing some dishes.

"Hello, sleepy-head," she smiled. "I was beginning to think you were in a coma."

She was shocked as he threw his arms around her and hugged her to him, crushing her with the intensity of his emotion. She could feel him trembling as he whispered: "I thought I'd lost you."

"Darling, you must have had a nasty dream. You know I'll never leave you," she comforted him.

Her words and her presence allayed his fears and Ian suddenly felt rather stupid. However, a few minutes later, his mood lightened and soon he was more like his normal self.

"No more beer at lunchtime, if that's what it does to me!" he laughed.

That night their love-making was more subdued, though very intense. He clung to Jane again as he had done earlier, wanting somehow to convince himself that, as she had said, she would never leave him. Afterwards, sleep would not come. For the first time since they had moved into the house a month before he felt uneasy. Something was bothering him, but he didn't know what it was.

He dozed fitfully, his mind far too busy for sleep to take him, until eventually, as dawn broke and the birds in the woods started their amazing chorus, he slipped quietly out of the bed. For a moment or two he stood looking at Jane. She slept on, her lovely face untroubled.

Ian dressed quietly, went down the stairs, and let himself out of the back door of the house into the garden. For a little while he stood there, drinking in the pure morning air, the music of the birdlife, the sheer pleasure of his surroundings. Then the thoughts which had kidnapped his sleep began to return, and a little shiver ran through him, though maybe it was the chill of the early morning.

Climbing the low fence at the end of the garden, he dropped onto the path which ran to the rear of the houses, through the wood and, eventually, down to the river. This morning, however, some strange intuition led him away from his normal route and on to another path, which led away to his right, towards the wood at the rear of the main golf club building. Much work was still in progress on the site and the finishing touches were still being applied to the conversion of the old Manor House into a luxurious clubhouse.

It was a magnificent old building of red sandstone, and its renovation, after years of neglect, was revealing how elegant it must have looked centuries ago, when it was the family seat of the lords of the manor.

Ian had never had any great sense for, or love of, history but there was a "feel" to the place which moved him, and which he could not explain. It was as if he had been destined to live here, as if the whole of his life to date had served only to bring him to this beautiful place.

The winding route of the path eventually brought him to the rear of the clubhouse. The developers had here retained the original layout of the gardens, and colourful beds of flowers lay symmetrically between stone-flagged paths, interspersed with ornamental ponds and sandstone statues, these much weathered and ravaged by the passage of time. It was a splendidly tranquil spot and it was not difficult to imagine it as it must have been in its prime.

Only one thing seemed out of place in the otherwise perfect layout.

At the end of the garden nearest to the wood was an area about sixteen feet square, enclosed by wrought iron railings about three feet high. Within this enclosure was an octagonal plinth which rose in three steps to about the same height as the railings. It was obviously the base for some statue or monument, though one much bigger than any of those present. As he stood looking at the plinth, Ian became aware of another presence and, turning to his right, saw a man approaching him.

"You're about bright and early, sir," said the approaching figure. "Can I help you with anything?".

"No, everything's fine," replied Ian. "I'm just out for an early morning stroll and I hadn't been this way before. I live in one of the new houses along the path there."

He pointed in the direction of his home, feeling like a guilty child caught stealing apples.

"I hope I'm not in trouble, but the path leads into here and I just followed it."

"No, sir, that's all right," said the man. "It will be fenced off when the job's finished, but for the time being they pay me to keep an eye on the place, I'm the night watchman. I was just on the point of knocking-off when I saw you."

"I'm sorry I've delayed you," Ian replied, "I'll be on my way and let you get to bed. Just one thing though, before you go, what's missing from here?"

He pointed to the plinth.

"Don't really know, sir, some religious relic I believe, it's locked up in the contractor's compound waiting for some decision to be made as to what they're going to do with it."

He made to turn away but Ian checked him again.

"What sort of relic, do you know?" he asked.

"Haven't seen it myself, so I can't swear to it, but they reckon it's a gravestone, something to do with the old Abbey days, but like I say, I'm not sure."

With this he turned away and, whistling softly, moved off down the path and into the wood.

For a few moments longer Ian stood in the same spot, looking at the plinth within the railings, and, as he did, that dreadful feeling of loss he had experienced the previous evening came creeping back into his mind.

Again, his thoughts turned to Jane and instantly he turned and ran. He fled down the path, scrambled over the fence into his garden and let himself into the house, then scrambled as fast as he could up the stairs to the bedroom.

The door was open and the bed was empty. The room seemed to float around him and a great wave of remorse washed over him. He was certain that his Janie had gone and a low moan escaped from his throat. Then he heard, as if through a pillow, Jane's voice, singing, and the sound of water playing against the shower curtains in the adjoining bathroom. The relief was immense, and he slumped onto the bed, crying into his pillow, unable to understand why, on two occasions now, he had been absolutely certain that his love was lost forever.

As he lay there the sleep that had eluded him all night finally caught up with him. When Jane emerged from the bathroom a quarter of an hour later he was out to the world. She smiled and kissed him gently, then went down the stairs to make his breakfast.

Chapter Seven

Ida stood naked in her little cell, carrying out her morning toilet, washing herself with the cold water and rough soap provided for that purpose. With the improvement in her health her young body had filled out again and as she looked down the length of it she was not displeased at what she saw. Her breasts were firm and heavy in the full bloom of youth, her full, strong hips complimented the slimness of her waist, and her legs were long and well shaped. She remembered the odd occasions, back in the village, when some of the older and bolder of the lads had followed her into the woods, eager to better their acquaintances with her.

Though older than she in years, their youthful fumblings had merely served to fuel the awakening desires she had felt, and she had relished the power she held over them, a power founded on her looks and the position her mother had held in their minds.

One in particular, bigger and bolder than the rest, had cornered her one day in the copse of silver birch as she searched for herbs. He had thrown her to the ground, his hot breath foul in her face, his hands on her breasts, pinching and kneading. Then the rough fingers between her legs, probing, hurting, the stab of pain as she was penetrated. She had screamed then and her mother had appeared as if from nowhere, the stick she carried crashing down on the youth's back. He had yelped in pain and fled in terror with the old woman's curses ringing in his ears.

The next day he had fallen from a tree whilst climbing. His legs were broken and he had never walked properly again. Ida remembered now that he had failed to survive the plague. As these thoughts went through her mind she thought for the first time of the old lady and the village she had left behind. These memories strengthened her resolve never again to be the plaything of any man, never to submit, without resistance, to their demands and lusts.

The rough door swung open and Ida turned, expecting to see

Sister Catherine. Instead she saw another, Sister Ambrose. She reached for her shift and covered herself, but not before she noticed the widening of Sister Ambrose's eyes, the sharp intake of breath and the tongue licking the thick lips. The eyes never left Ida's body and the face, by nature ruddy, now flushed bright red as the blood flowed to it. The older woman reached out to touch Ida and the girl stepped back, now aware of the desire that showed itself in this woman's face, that same carnal lechery she had seen in the eyes of the village lad.

"Hush now, my little one," said the older woman. "I know all your secrets, and now I want you to share mine."

"What do you mean, my secrets?" Ida cried. "I have no secrets."

"What about the old priest, what happened to him? Who killed him? What happened to them? How did they die: who started the fire? In your sleep you have said much, and I have listened. Sister Catherine knows too, but she will tell no-one. We share your secret, but with a difference. She will say nothing because she is a good woman and cares greatly for you. My silence must be bought. I am not as other women."

Ida shrank down onto her little cot, not fully understanding, yet dreadfully aware of the desire in the other's eyes. She flinched as the shift was snatched from her grasp, leaving her naked body exposed to view. She cringed as the nun leaned over her, feeling the hot breath against her face and the bony fingers digging cruelly into her breasts and thighs. With a sob of disgust she hit out at the probing hands and leering face, and the ferocity of her attack momentarily drove Sister Ambrose back. However the older woman was much bigger and more heavily built and, after her initial shock, she quickly regained the upper hand. Now she pinned Ida down on the cot and once again the bony fingers went to work, scratching and kneading, forcing their way into Ida's body, hurting her, inflicting such pain and shame as she had never felt before.

The assault seemed to go on for ages and soon the girl ceased to resist, not daring to scream, realising the futility of it. At last the older woman rose, her face ugly now and flushed with triumph,

34

her upper lip and brow beaded with sweat, the lust she felt still gleaming in her eyes.

"Tonight I will come to you again, my pretty one. Tell no-one of this or your secret will be out. The sheriff's men will take you to the castle and they know how to handle pretty young killers like you."

She stroked Ida's belly once more then turned and left, closing the door quietly behind her.

For a long time Ida remained on the cot, body and mind abused, incapable of coherent thought, yet knowing that this morning was only a taste of what she could expect from this woman who literally held her life in those cruel, searching fingers. Slowly she rose from the bed then went back to her toilet.

She scrubbed at her skin till it was sore, trying to wash away the degradation, the filth which she felt had tainted her body. This had not been like the boy in the wood, this had been different – depraved, dirty, unnatural. She burned with shame and anger and already her mind was beginning to seek an escape from this latest danger, a defence against this evil. She dressed then, and went out into the convent gardens, thus avoiding contact with any of the other nuns who she knew would now be at morning service.

Alone in the garden a plan began to form in her mind. She must rid herself of this woman and her foul practice, and the fact that it was a secret must be to her advantage. If no-one knew of the liaison then no-one could suspect Ida if anything were to happen to Sister Ambrose. But the plan must be carefully thought through, she could afford to take no chances, and she steeled herself to accept that she must, perforce, suffer further abuse until such time as she was ready to act. But act she must, just as she had been moved to avenge the old priest, she had no illusions about that.

That night, as the door to her cell swung open, her initial plans suffered a severe setback as not just one, but two figures entered. In the half-light Ida could make out that the newcomer was Sister Martine. As she looked up at the two women, Ida recalled having seen them together a lot. They worked together in the gardens and went out together on the days when visits were made into the city. In fact, when she came to think about it, she realised she had seldom seen one of them without the other being in close proximity.

The newcomer said nothing but went immediately to the business in hand. Her hands, though equally rough-skinned as her partner's, were more gentle, coaxing and stroking, fingertips subtly playing around Ida's nipples until, resist as she might, she felt herself becoming aroused. As the moistness spread between her legs an involuntary little moan escaped from her throat, and at this, Sister Ambrose, who until then had stood watching, now put her hands and mouth to work on the girl.

Ida writhed and twisted but the combined weight of the two women was more than she could resist and the skilled hands, working in tandem on her body, brought her very quickly to a sexual climax. She moaned softly and her body heaved in orgasm as the two performed their practised skills on her. As Ida fell back, spent, they turned their attentions away from her and to each other, and the girl watched in disgust as each abused the other in an orgy of sexual degradation.

When it was over and they had gone, Ida lay on her bed, once more turning her tortured thoughts to finding a solution to her dilemma. One answer would be to simply leave the convent, but she knew that without money she would struggle to survive, and, if Sister Ambrose carried out her threat to tell of her past, she would be quickly arrested and imprisoned.

To leave the city itself would be even more hazardous. The plague was not yet over and she knew from bitter experience that her long-term chances of survival outside the convent and city would only be slim. No, leaving was not the answer, she must stay and fight.

She heard a scratching noise at the door and she gasped in fear that the two women were returning, but, as the door slowly swung open, it revealed the figure of the large black cat she had last seen on the day she left the village. It jumped effortlessly up onto the cot and rubbed its great head against her body, a deep growling purr rumbling in its throat. She clasped it to her, stroking and fondling its smooth bulk, gaining great comfort from its presence. Soon, she slept, a sleep surprisingly untroubled and deep.

She awoke early the next day and the cat had vanished. At first she wondered if she had dreamed of its presence the night before. Then she found, on the rough pillow, a single, long, black whisker and knew that she had not been imagining things. The cat had actually come to her, and, with it, the answer to her problem began to form in her mind.

Memories of her mother seemed to stir and grow. Moving pictures formed in her head, and then she felt the presence of the old woman, in her mind, guiding her very thoughts. She rose from the cot and quickly dressed, her body still aching from the previous night's ordeal. The pain served to steel her resolve and, leaving her cell she went into the garden, where some impulse guided her feet to a little pile of stones and rubble heaped against the wall. Without really knowing why, she picked up a stick and began to root amongst the stones with it. As she turned one of the larger stones there was a movement beneath it and from its shelter emerged a huge toad.

Instantly, Ida knew. Her mother's voice came back to her: "Take a toad and place it in a sack with salt. Shake it well to anger it, two days, use the salt for giving to men."

She remembered the woman leaving their house in the village clutching the little sack of salt her mother had given her, and the death, a few weeks later, of the woman's husband, a man much older than she, and crippled by rheumatism. She recalled, too, that the woman had subsequently re-married a much younger and wealthier man.

At the time Ida had not connected the visit of the woman to her mother with the subsequent death of her man, but now it all became clear to her. The sequence of events had not been coincidental.

She bent and picked up the toad, feeling its fat, warty body squirm and wriggle as she gripped it. Returning to her little room she placed it beneath an upturned wooden bowl, out of sight underneath the cot. Later that morning she visited the kitchen and stole a handful of salt, and during the afternoon she made a little cloth sack; her preparations were now complete.

That evening they came again to Ida's cell, twins of evil, each seeking to outdo the other in their debauchery. They seemed insatiable, and her half-stifled moans of pain and humiliation seemed only to spur them on to even greater depths of depravity. When they eventually departed Ida was again left bruised and bleeding, her senses deadened by their lasciviousness.

She lay for a long time after they left, then, slowly and painfully rose from the cot and from beneath it withdrew the bowl and the toad, the bag she had made and the packet of salt she had hidden. She placed the ugly creature in the bowl and sprinkled a little of the salt over it, together with a few drops of water.

The reaction was immediate. The warty skin of the toad began to exude tiny beads of moisture, as though the creature was sweating. This moisture picked up more of the salt and the process was repeated, the toad now beginning to squirm and struggle, scrabbling at the sides of the bowl in an attempt to escape the torment. At this point Ida took the little sack she had made and into it placed the toad and the rest of the stolen salt. She shook the sack well, then tied it at the neck and returned it to the hiding place beneath the cot.

As she took to her bed that night a grim little smile played about her lips, but her eyes were cold and hard.

"Now we shall fight back," she murmured, and went to sleep.

Chapter Eight

The watchman's story had intrigued Ian and he determined to find out more about the old Abbey and the mysterious missing gravestone. Someone in the area must know more than the watchman had revealed, and Ian began to make his enquiries. The majority of the residents of the new estate had moved, like he, into the area from further afield and his questions bore little fruit, most people only having heard snatches of stories or vague rumours. That evening Ian decided to return to Hartford Hall, there to pump old George for anything more he might know.

The old man was less than cooperative, reluctant to discuss the subject.

"Let it go, lad," he pleaded with Ian. "No good can come of it, leave things be, please."

However Ian was not to be put off and continued to badger him until finally the barman gave in.

"I can tell you very little you don't already know," he said, "but the subject is widely covered in the library in Northwich. There's been any number of books written about it. They'll tell you what you want to know, but I still think you should leave things alone.".

Ian's mind was made up, however and he was determined to visit the library at the earliest opportunity. George's repeated warnings and reticence had only served to sharpen his appetite for knowledge. As he sat in the bar his eyes turned once more to the sign, "The Nun's Suite", and he smiled.

"Yes, my fine lady, I'm going to find out all about you!"

How much he was to find out, he didn't then know...

Chapter Nine

When, two tortured nights and days later, Ida had emptied the contents of the sack into the bowl, the toad's skin was broken and slimy, weeping from a mass of sores, and the salt had soaked up its secretions, absorbing its toxins. She had washed the toad and returned it to its hiding place, thanking it, as she did so, for its gift. Secretly, she had managed to dry the damp and now discoloured salt in the kitchen and she now carried it with her in a little packet, wherever she went. Her first opportunity to administer the poison, for that was what she now carried, came a few days later.

Sister Martine was at work in the small vegetable garden. The day was warm, and hoeing and weeding was thirsty work. As Ida passed, the older woman looked up from her work.

"Bring me some water, pretty one," she said. "Be a good girl for me, and tonight you shall have your reward."

She laughed evilly at her own joke. Ida merely nodded, then turned away.

"And soon you shall have yours," she murmured beneath her breath.

She found a pitcher and made her way to the well from which the convent's water supply was drawn. She drew a bucket of water and poured some into the pitcher, then added a good pinch of the salt to it. She took the merest taste herself, and was satisfied that nothing obvious could be detected. She carried the jug and a cup to the garden.

"Pour me a cup, little one, and take one yourself, join me in slaking this thirst as you have joined us in slaking our other thirst."

She laughed cruelly then raised the cup to her lips and drank long and deeply of the water, the fingers which Ida had grown to hate holding the cup to her mouth, the evil mouth sucking at the cup as it had sucked at Ida's body. She knew that the girl was watching her and she laughed again, her thoughts on the night ahead.

But that night they did not come. At evening prayers, only Sister

40

Ambrose had been present. Ida learned from Sister Catherine that Sister Martine had taken to her bed complaining of stomach cramps, and was feeling rather unwell. Ida took her old benefactor to one side.

"You know something of my past, good Sister, and of the potions I brought from the village. I have a remedy for stomach pains. I will mix some for you to take to our Sister."

She returned to her cell and took from her pack a small bottle. As she removed the stopper the sweet smell of peppermint pervaded the cell. She let a few drops of it fall into a mixing bowl then sat for a few moments sorting through the other jars and packets.

There was wolfbane, which she knew would take away the pain but add to the poison; belladonna, also good for the stomach pain but again, used in excess, a poison; the various dried fungi, death cap, fly agaric and destroying angel; all of them deadly, all of them added, a tiny pinch at a time, to the bowl.

More of the toad salt followed and, as an afterthought, several more drops of the sweet-smelling peppermint. She ground and stirred the ingredients together and added some water to the cocktail which she then took to Sister Catherine.

"Take this to Sister Ambrose – she can give a little to Sister Martine and she will find some comfort from the pain. But tell them nothing of me. I know that many people do not accept my mother's ways and fear me because of it," she said.

"Bless you, my child," the old woman smiled, "I will tell them nothing, but God will know and He shall reward you for your benevolence."

The girl smiled and turned away.

"Aye, that He will," she thought, "but not in the way you believe."

The days passed and Sister Martine grew weaker as the poisons worked their way into her system. True, the pains receded as the narcotic drugs did their work, but the toxins, too, went about their deadly business, their presence undetectable beneath the strong smell and taste of the peppermint.

In less than two weeks it was over. During this time Ida had remained unmolested while Sister Ambrose tended her lover. She had watched, hard-eyed, as Sister Ambrose daily administered the poison, feeling no guilt, no pity, no remorse. Already her mind was working on the next problem, that of getting rid of Sister Ambrose, who, she had no doubt, would resume her practices with Ida at the earliest opportunity.

They had gathered in the crypt deep beneath the convent, a small group of nuns, to pay their last respects to their departed sister. At the graveside Sister Ambrose, weeping copiously, watched as the simple coffin was lowered into the shallow grave beneath the flagstones, the Mother Superior's prayers going out to the Maker, the bell tolling in the chapel above, sending out its message of death over the bowed heads of the gathered throng.

Sister Ambrose raised her eyes and saw, directly opposite, her head unbowed, the tall straight figure of Ida, a grim smile on the lovely young face, and in that instant came the dreadful realisation of how her lover had died.

Chapter Ten

For the first time since the honeymoon, Ian had taken a few days off work. Jane had announced that she thought she was pregnant, and, a few days later, their doctor had confirmed the fact. It was hardly a surprise to either of them as they had taken few precautions during their love-making. Even so, the news took a little getting used to. They were both thrilled and excited at the thought of being parents, and that evening celebrated by getting mellowly drunk with a bottle of champagne followed by an early retirement to bed, where, if it had not already been the case, Jane would certainly have stood a very good chance of conceiving.

A few days later Jane had an appointment at the ante-natal clinic in town and afterwards they went to do a little shopping. As they passed the library, Ian was reminded of George's advice regarding his desire for information. Jane wanted some time to herself around the shops and was happy to agree when Ian suggested they should meet later in the library reading-room. He had told Jane something of what he had discovered, including his discovery of the monument and his meeting with the watchman, and she knew that he was set on finding out more, so humoured his wishes.

The librarian at the information desk was extremely helpful and Ian was soon settled at a table with a couple of books she had kindly pointed out to him. As he read, he began to appreciate the historical significance of the site on which their home now stood.

He read a little about the construction of the magnificent Abbey in the thirteenth and fourteenth centuries. He flicked through the pages quickly, not really absorbing what he read, looking for something else, yet not knowing what. Then, in a book published by a local history society, he came across a conjectural plan, based on two lots of excavations carried out earlier in the century, the first in 1912 and the second in 1958.

According to this plan, where the high altar would have stood, and surrounded on three sides by thirteen chapels, he saw the words "The Nun's Grave." He felt a little thrill of excitement, but also a gut feeling of apprehension. At last some of the answers to the mystery were beginning to fall into place, but, as they did, more questions were posed.

Turning again to the books on the table he read more about the Abbey. It had been of the Cistercian order, an especially strict form of the Benedictine rule. In the books he found no other mention of nuns or a convent nearby. Why, then, should there be a nun's grave in this bastion of male dominance, and why should it be so situated, in such an exalted position, near the High Altar? Who had this mystery nun been, to warrant so esteemed a position in the scheme of things?

His thoughts were interrupted by Jane's arrival, and he replaced the books on the shelves, determined to return the next time an opportunity presented itself. He was very quiet on the journey home, which prompted Jane to ask:

"Did you find what you were looking for, love?".

"Not exactly," he replied. "There's much more to this Nun business than meets the eye. But I will get to the bottom of it, if it's the last thing I do."

Chapter Eleven

etween Ida and Sister Ambrose an undeclared truce existed. The death of her lover had deeply affected the older woman, and, to a certain extent, scared her. She only now ate and drank in the company of the other nuns, watching particularly the serving platters from which Ida and her mentor Sister Catherine ate, and choosing her food from those. She knew now that Sister Martine had been poisoned, yet had no recourse to justice or law, because of her "special" relationship with her. Neither the Church nor the judiciary, at that time, had any sympathy for what were considered to be unlawful and unnatural practices, sinful in the eyes of God. Yet she was determined to take her revenge on Ida, but in a way which must not put herself in any danger, and could not be traced back to her.

She would bide her time and wait for an opportunity to present itself.

For her part, Ida was content, for the time being, to let matters rest. The nocturnal visits had ceased with the death of Sister Martine and Ida had noted, with satisfaction, the fear and hatred in the eyes of Sister Ambrose whenever they came face to face. She now had no fear of the older woman, but knew, instinctively, that danger was never far away and that she must, at all times, maintain her vigilance.

Life in the convent had now very much returned to normal. The plague seemed to have completed its dreadful harvest, no deaths and no further outbreaks having been discovered for several weeks. Activities in the city, too, were starting to resume their previous patterns. Shops re-opened and such surviving street traders as there were, began once again to make their voices heard. The streets were cleared of the litter and filth which had accumulated over several months, repairs were started on the properties which had fallen victim to the looters, and those same looters were rounded up and thrown into the city prison.

A general feeling of thankfulness and well-being spread

through the community at large, and this was echoed in the religious community in particular, with services of thanks to God for His mercy and deliverance from those terrible times, now hopefully behind them.

As normality was restored, communications with the outside world were re-established as traders and travellers began, once more, to appear at the great city gates. The news they brought was grim. The whole area had been decimated, whole communities wiped out, in some villages not a soul was left alive. They told of many incidents, like that witnessed by Ida, of robbery, rape and murder, of roaming bands of cut-throats and cattle thieves. It was not safe to travel alone and many of the travellers had banded together for mutual protection, moving only when their numbers were sufficient to deter attack. Some of the merchants had recruited bodyguards, mercenaries who hired out to the highest bidder and whose allegiance was only to gold.

Ready as she was to move on, Ida decided that the time was not yet right. She would stay a little longer in the convent, building up her strength and reserves before making the break.

Apart from her devotion to old Sister Catherine, there was little to hold her to the place. She had no more contact with the other sisters than her duties necessitated, and took little part in the religious aspects of life in the convent. She was tolerated, in spite of this, for her considerable physical strength, which, allied to her powers of healing through her knowledge of the natural medicines she used, placed her in great demand. Of these gifts she gave generously, nursing many of the city's sick with a devotion far greater than her status demanded, building a reputation for benevolence far beyond her just deserts.

To the wretched poor of the city, especially the smaller children, she took what food the nuns could spare. She washed and cared for the little ones, cleaning and wrapping their festering sores, setting broken bones, mixing and administering her ointments and powders to all in need.

As Ida's reputation and popularity grew, so did the loathing in the heart of Sister Ambrose. That this bitch, who had murdered her friend and lover, could be held in such adulation by the people, was like a goad, pricking her hatred, stirring it to a seething animus of the girl and her very existence. To Sister Ambrose the need for vengeance became an obsession; no matter what became of herself, this girl must die.

But first she must suffer...

Chapter Twelve

an's research was sporadic, his progress slow. Jane's pregnancy was not going easily. In the early stages things had been fine, but then had come the morning sickness and with it a drastic change in her mental attitude. She had become resentful and protective, rejecting his attempts to comfort her, brushing away his hands as he tried to touch her swelling body. Their lovemaking had ceased totally, all his approaches rejected out of hand. She said it was for the good of the baby, though she was barely four months into the pregnancy. It was, to Ian, like living with a total stranger, and all the more hurtful because of their previous freedom and lack of inhibition. It was as if Jane was trying to drive him away, alienate his feelings towards her, keep him away from her and the baby.

He took to wandering alone through the woods and along the riverbank, exploring, discovering many things he had not previously known existed. He found the remains of an old wooden building, rotting and overgrown, hidden deep in the undergrowth near the water's edge. An old boathouse, perhaps, though not of any great antiquity, certainly it could not have survived since the Abbey times. Here and there were great blocks of sandstone, sometimes alone, sometimes in numbers.

"Could these be part of the original Abbey?" he asked himself. The large stones from which the nearby locks and weirs on the river were constructed, were of a different material, much harder than sandstone, which could not itself have survived the action of the water for centuries. Just lying about in the woods though, and half buried or sheltered by the trees, these great blocks could easily, he supposed, have survived through the ages and could, indeed, be part of the ruins of that once magnificent edifice he had read about.

Apart from his particular interest in the mysterious tale of the nun, he found that he was becoming drawn deeper and deeper into the general history of the area. He was becoming increasingly aware of the former importance of this place where he now lived, and, strangely enough, felt an increasing pride in his involvement.

History had never been one of his favourite subjects, but this was different, this was somehow real and alive, that here amongst these trees and fields, over seven hundred years ago, there had existed a great religious establishment, where men had worked and worshipped, lived and died.

So it was, that, as Jane became more distant and withdrawn, Ian, in his ignorance, accepted it, engrossing himself in his work and his new obsession with the past.

Winter was fast approaching and as the weeks passed Jane became increasingly morose and detached. Her moods now varied little, ranging from ill-tempered outbursts to long periods of silence, alarmingly at odds with those of her pre-pregnancy days. She resented Ian's absences yet rebuffed any attempts he made at reconciliation, few as these were now becoming. The life inside her became her only concern. This was her baby and she felt she could share it with no-one. Her trips to the clinics had become an ordeal, the questions, the probing, the scans: why couldn't they all just leave her alone to look after her baby her own way? Her barely concealed anger did not go un-noticed by those she met, and their concern was expressed to Ian. He, however, had seemingly become inured to the situation and brushed aside their questions with a shrug of indifference, saying:

"She'll be all right when the baby comes. It's just the strain of everything at the moment. She says she prefers to be alone, so why all the fuss?"

Reluctantly, the medical staff and the few friends they had made were forced to accept Ian's philosophical approach. Jane was, after all, physically sound and the baby perfectly normal. Perhaps, as her husband said, it was just a bit of stress because of her condition.

For his own part, Ian was content to continue his search for more information about the mysterious monument at the rear of the clubhouse and its unknown occupant. Further visits to the library had confirmed that the grave of a nun had existed on the site in mediaeval times, but nowhere could he find a satisfactory explanation as to why.

During his visits he had met several local historians, some of whom had written books of their own on various aspects of the area, yet none of these was seemingly prepared to proffer any specific assistance on this particular subject. They would talk for hours on the salt and chemical industries which had been the mainstay of the town for years, they would tell of its floods and subsidence, of buildings which had disappeared into the bowels of the earth, of old pubs, shops and market halls, but of Vale Royal and its Nun's Grave they knew little, or, if they did, were keeping it to themselves. Each time he broached the subject he became increasingly aware of this reluctance to become involved.

He remembered again old George's advice to leave things be, an attitude seemingly adopted by these people generally. The subject seemed to be taboo and this angered and frustrated him, hardening still further his determination to get to the bottom of the mystery. His interest had by now become almost an obsession, his mind oblivious to the crisis building up in his marriage and to his wife's illness. Though he could not see it, his marriage was under serious threat, his wife in danger.

Chapter Thirteen

It was the beginning of March and in the convent preparations were in progress to celebrate the Feast Day of St. Benedict, the founder of their great Order. Custom had it that representatives of the churches, monasteries, convents and priories in the area would assemble, at a chosen place, on the designated day each year. This year, with the passing of the plague, those spared had much to celebrate and many to mourn.

It was decreed that the celebrations should last for a two full weeks culminating on the date of the Feast Day, the twenty-first of the month, thus allowing ample time for all concerned to express, in their prayers, gratitude to The Lord for their deliverance. Because of the added importance of this particular year, made so memorable by the shocking losses caused by the plague, it was further decreed that the celebrations would be hosted by the White Monks resident at the largest and most important of the Order's establishments, the great Cistercian Abbey of St. Mary at Vale Royal.

This constituted, for the nuns from Chester, a journey of about twenty miles, too far for some of the older and frailer ones to possibly undertake. The Mother Superior and her elders had conferred and drawn up a list of who was to travel and who must stay behind. To Ida's delight she was one of those chosen to make the journey.

For a while now she had felt the urge to get away from the constrictions of the convent, to experience once more the freedom to walk in fields, amongst trees, as she had in her village as a child. Though only a few months had gone by since her arrival, it seemed to her like years ago. As she heard the names read out her pleasure was marred somewhat to learn that Sister Catherine would not be going on the journey, but her own excitement far outweighed her disappointment. She knew from her own experiences that the decision was a sensible one, for the ordeal would surely prove too much for the frail old nun.

51

She remembered her own terrible journey from the village to the city and knew that the one they were about to undertake was even longer, and likely to be equally arduous. Her youthful vigour and strength had weighed heavily in her favour when the convent elders had made their decision. There were some who had argued against her inclusion, on the grounds that she was only, as yet, a novice, and a reluctant one at that, but even they were forced to agree that she would, indeed, be an asset on the trip if only for her physical presence.

So Ida was assigned the task of organising and arranging such transport as could be found. Ten of the nuns, including Ida, would be in the party to travel to Vale Royal, leaving only four and a couple of novices to carry on the work at St. Mary's. Of these ten, several, including the Mother Superior, were somewhat elderly and quite incapable of making the journey on foot, so some means of transport must be provided for them.

During the worst ravages of the plague, the sisters had done much to help the inhabitants of the city, often at great cost to themselves. Now came the chance for the people of the city to reward them for their sacrifice. One grateful merchant offered the use of a covered cart, together with an ancient and weary-looking horse. Another came up with a pair of pack horses, equally time-worn but, nevertheless, gladly accepted by Ida.

Her transport requirements now satisfied, she began to accumulate provisions for the trip, dried and salted meats and fish, a small sack of vegetables, some eggs and a goose, anything she could beg from the people of the city. So popular was she that the sisters' needs for their pilgrimage were soon satisfied. With only one exception, her colleagues were unstinting in their praise of her efforts.

To Sister Ambrose, each smile and compliment given to Ida was like the twist of a knife in her wounded senses. Her hatred grew daily more intense, more vicious, fed by her sexual frustration and jealousy. She had considered and discarded numerous schemes to kill Ida, none of them feasible without risk to herself, and as each plan was rejected it added further to her torment. As the day of the journey drew nearer, she began to consider other ways of hurting the girl, and the solution came to her suddenly and quite simply. She watched as Ida walked through the grounds with Sister Catherine, their heads bowed together in conversation. She saw the look of affection on the girl's face as she talked, the little touch of her hand on the old woman's arm, and the response it solicited from her.

There was the answer staring her in the face. Why had she not seen it before? The old woman, Ida's friend, must die, as her own friend had died. Then the girl would know the hurt she was feeling, suffer as she was suffering, until the time when the ultimate revenge could be taken. To her crazed mind the idea was brilliant, kill the one to torture the other, and then, when the chance arose, kill again. In that way there would be twice the pleasure, twice the satisfaction, and disposing of the old woman should present few problems.

From the hatching of the plan to its moment of execution took only two days.

Sister Catherine laboured slowly to the top of the steps which led up to the walkway round the city walls. From her vantage point some eighty feet above the River Dee she gazed down on the old stone bridge, its arches spanning the water as they had since Roman times. As she paused to regain her breath after the exhausting ascent, she wondered ruefully how much longer she would be able to carry on this work, climb these steps; how many more times she would be afforded the pleasure of this view. She was almost eighty years old, lucky to have survived the plague, for which she had thanked her God, and growing weaker by the day. Many of her daily tasks had been taken over by Ida and she smiled as she thought of the youngster, her willingness to help, her eagerness to please. She had brought a brightness to Sister Catherine's life such as she had not known for many years. She smiled again in genuine pleasure at the thought.

It was fitting that the last thoughts of this gracious old woman should be happy ones. Sister Ambrose stepped from her hiding place behind a nearby buttress and, with one savage heave, despatched the old woman to her Maker. The frail body turned over and over in the air before crunching sickeningly into the cobblestones far below, but by then the murderess had vanished, unseen.

They brought the poor, broken body to the nunnery an hour or so later. No-one had seen her fall but a passerby had found the body and notified a constable. In his strong arms she had the appearance of a small child and as the news spread and the nuns gathered in the small courtyard, it was Ida who stepped forward to take her from him.

The tears flowed down her face unchecked and a sob burst from her throat. She carried her old friend into the chapel, and there began to straighten the broken limbs and gently wipe away the blood from the tired face. Sister Catherine was dearly loved by all at the convent and her death shocked them all, but none more so than Ida. More than any other, she had come to love the old woman, and she wept at her loss.

Standing nearest to Ida, as she knelt by the body of her friend, was Sister Ambrose, hardly able to conceal her sadistic satisfaction at the pain on Ida's face. She covered her face with her hands in a pretence at tears, thus concealing her expression, but at the movement Ida glanced up. Through her tears she saw the blurred outline of Sister Ambrose and, with that animal-like instinct she possessed, instantly penetrated the facade of sympathy. She wiped the tears from her face and stared, long and hard, at Sister Ambrose. Sister Ambrose gloatingly tried to hold her stare, return it, but after a few seconds she realised she was looking into the face of Death and backed away, whimpering now for real, terror in her heart.

Because of the imminence of the planned journey, the funeral service had to be hurriedly arranged and took place the next morning. It was the usual simple ceremony accorded the members of the Sisterhood, and attended only by them and the parish priest. Quietly and reverentially Sister Catherine was laid to rest, and in ones and twos the sisters moved away from the graveside and out of the crypt till only Ida was left. As she knelt at the scene, gazing down at the simple coffin in the as yet unfilled grave she made a silent vow: "Rest easy, little mother, you shall be avenged. For the evil one there shall be no rest, no peace, till justice is done. This I swear."

For a moment longer she stayed, head bowed, then stood and walked away. Now there were no tears, just a grim set to the young jaw, a hard, cold look in the eyes.

All around the county, travel arrangements were being made for the great day. At each of the Order's establishments carts and pack animals were being loaded, and some of those from the more distant areas were, indeed, already on their way along the roads and tracks converging on the Abbey at Vale Royal.

One such group was a small party of monks from the northern boundary of the county. Norton Priory stood on a sandstone bluff, high above the mudflats of the River Mersey. A recently established subordinate of Vale Royal, its members were few, a prior, six monks and a number of lay brethren, the labourers of the Order, many of whom were uneducated, some petty criminals, who had taken up the cloth as sanctuary from the law and a source of food and shelter.

This was a situation common to many of the religious establishments of the time, when justice could be extremely hard and punishments excessively cruel.

One member of the Norton party who was in such a predicament, was John of Dutton. Son of a poor herdsman who worked for the local lord, he had been forced to flee his home after stealing milk from that nobleman's shippon. The fact that he had been close to starving at the time elicited no sympathy, and a flogging was the least he could expect if caught. He had been seen and identified and, rather than face that cruel punishment, had fled.

He had subsequently been taken in by the brothers of Norton, given food and clothing, and in exchange had proved a willing and useful hand in the gardens of the Priory. As was the case with Ida at Chester, his great physical prowess and eagerness to help had won him favour with his new masters. This trip was, therefore, partly a reward for his efforts, but, more to the point, a shrewd assessment of his value to his fellow travellers in terms of workrate.

As he strode along beside the cart carrying three of the older monks, his mind was abuzz with excitement. Like so many of his status, he had rarely travelled far from the place he had been born, and this was, to him, a great adventure.

So it was that, as the day drew on, from all points of the compass, little bands of pilgrims began to converge on the great Abbey at Vale Royal.

Chapter Fourteen

A t last Ian had got to see the missing parts of the monument. Over the weeks he had gained the confidence of the watchman, who had eventually been persuaded to let him into the contractor's compound at the rear of the hall where the remains were being stored.

There were two sections to the upright part of the monument, laid out side by side on the ground. The headpiece of the gravestone consisted of a an open sided cube containing four small statuettes. It was much worn by the ravages of time and the figures were very indistinct. Topping the cube was a cross. This part of the relic was obviously of great antiquity. Not so the main shaft of the monument, on which the headpiece had obviously stood. About six feet high and carved from one piece of sandstone, it was quite plain that it was contemporary to the present building and was therefore not a part of the original shrine. Comparing these two parts with the base in the grounds it was furthermore apparent that this too was different, more reminiscent of the great blocks of stone he had discovered in the surrounding woods and near the river.

So, though he was no expert in masonry or architecture, it appeared to Ian that the gravestone, if indeed it was such, was made up of three distinct parts from widely differing periods, with one piece, the cross, of different stone from the other two.

The mystery deepened and Ian's curiosity was further stimulated. From his research, he had discovered that the original Abbey had been constructed over a period of some fifty years, between its foundation in 1277 and the date of the first monks being transferred there in 1330. He had also found out that the Abbey had not survived the Reformation of the early sixteenth century, when, under the rule of Henry VIII, it had been dismantled and its stones used in the building of new churches in the surrounding area.

Why, then, had this gravestone, a monument to a nun, survived for over four hundred years longer than the Abbey itself?

Was this woman so important, so powerful, that her memory outlived that of the monks who had occupied the site for almost three hundred years and of whom there was so little trace? And, if such was the case, why could he now find out so little about her?

Excavations in 1958, he had read, had revealed the remains of over twenty bodies, one headless, but no gravestones or markers. These remains had been found concentrated in one communal area outside the walls of the Abbey and certain artifacts found amongst them revealed that they were the bodies of monks. The method of laying out the bodies, too, was typical of the Order, laid due east to west, head against the transept wall, with the right arm flexed across the chest and the left by the side, slightly bent at the elbow.

So, then, the monks were buried outside the walls but this mystery nun had achieved a place of great favour, not merely inside the Abbey, but at the site of the High Altar. What, Ian wondered, had her status been, that she should be accorded so great an honour? He felt he was no nearer solving the mystery now than when he first came across it.

Jane, in the meantime, remained isolated from him. She had withdrawn more and more into herself and her forthcoming baby, and Ian's pursuit of the answer to the mystery failed to interest her in the slightest. If he wished to spend every minute of his spare time rooting about in the woods or stuck in the reading room at the library, then so be it. She had her baby to come and could think of little else.

The sickness of the earlier months had passed and physically her health was much improved. Her doctor's concern was now almost entirely about her mental state. Although she was perfectly lucid and attentive in all matters concerning the forthcoming offspring, she had little interest in discussing anything else with him. He tried in various ways to discuss her marriage and to bring her to talk about Ian, but his efforts were of no avail and this worried him greatly. Although the couple were new to his practice, his first impressions of them had been favourable, and he had been pleased to impart the news to Jane of her pregnancy. On her earlier visits she was always accompanied by Ian, who was obviously as thrilled as she was at the news. But now she had taken to arriving alone and over three months had passed since the doctor had last seen him.

Although the situation greatly worried him, under the circumstances there was little the doctor could actually do to bring them back together. He resolved to monitor the situation as carefully as he was able, knowing in his mind that if it was allowed to go on unchecked, things could only get worse.

All reports on the baby were favourable, so in that area, at least, there was nothing to worry about. He could only hope that a similar state of affairs would soon be restored to the parents-to-be.

Chapter Fifteen

Not all the bands of robbers and murderers worked the border lands. As the defences along the border improved, easier pickings were to be found further east. Several of the gangs now operated freely throughout the county, moving quickly, hitting small villages and isolated homesteads at will.

In the ancient forest of Delamere which covered great tracts of Cheshire, many such gangs had established hideaways. The vast expanses of trees, interspersed by numerous trails, formed a labyrinth into which few pursuers would ever dare follow. Game was abundant and there were numerous streams and springs of fresh pure water. Farmland adjoined the forest edges and all the needs of the bandits could be easily satisfied. Still, however, they craved greater wealth.

From his position on the Pale Heights near Eddesbury, Morgan, leader of one of these bandit groups, could see his native mountains, some thirty miles distant to the west. His vantage point also afforded a view over much of the forest and sections of the tracks which wound through it.

For many months now he had led his pack of thugs as they raided the farms and villages of the surrounding area. They had robbed and pillaged, raped and burned, tortured and killed, returning afterwards to the haven of their hideout, near the old quarry workings deep in the heart of the forest. The band was five strong, his subordinates four of the most evil villains even he, Morgan, had ever come across.

Yet, even amongst such cutthroats, Morgan ruled by fear. He was a huge bull of a man, the black hair and beard of his race emphasising the darkness of his complexion. The same black hair covered most of his body and gave him the appearance of some wild animal. He was totally without fear, yet so easily inspired it in others.

Now he was discontented. Although they were living off the fat of the land, taking goods and women as the mood took them, what he really craved was gold, sufficient gold to buy him property of his own across the border, and a small army to defend it. Morgan had heard tell of a great feast day to be held at the Monastery of Vale Royal, and he could smell the gold.

His men had taken up vantage points throughout the forest. All the main tracks were under observation and should anything come their way he would soon be aware of it. His concentration was on one of the more important routes through the forest, that running from Chester, west of his position, to the salt-towns to the east. Pack trains carrying that precious cargo frequently travelled this track, but so well-guarded were they that attacks were very dangerous, as the gang had found out to their cost. Morgan apart, they were a pack of cowards with little stomach for a real fight, their preference being for lonely women and old men who put up little resistance.

As he watched the trail, Morgan mused long and hard about his situation. He was better than this scum he had surrounded himself with, he told himself, and with their help he intended soon to be rid of them. He would one day return to his home across the river and make a fresh start. But first he needed gold, and, from what he had heard, this could be the opportunity he was waiting for.

His information was that there was to be a great gathering of all the churches, nunneries and priories, under the one roof, and Morgan's theory was that, as they travelled, the monks and nuns would bring with them their artifacts of gold and silver.

He, Dewi Morgan, would join in their celebrations.

In the distance a movement caught his eye and, within a few minutes, he was able to make out a small group, a mixture of wagons, horses and people. Ten minutes later he could assess the strength of the party more accurately. It comprised just one small covered cart, a couple of pack mules or horses, and a dozen or so people, who, judging by their dress, could be female. This was the sort of target which appealed to Morgan, with little prospect of danger and, potentially easy rewards.

Watching the slow progress of the little group as they began the long ascent from the village of Kelsall towards the forest proper, he estimated it would take them at least another hour to reach the crossroads at the Chamber of the Forest, the spot where the four main trails through the great forest converged. This was to be his ambush point, and his lookouts were stationed at strategic positions throughout the forest covering each trail. Reaching for the horn at his belt he blew one long blast upon it, the signal for his men to assemble at the crossroads, then started down the hill. There was plenty of time to prepare a suitable reception for this group of pilgrims.

In the party below, Ida's keen hearing picked up the sound of the horn and some basic instinct warned her that danger was near. Since the start of their journey, as dawn had broken, her mind had been re-living her previous journey and its horrible events, together with the happenings of the last two days. The death and funeral of Sister Catherine had greatly affected her, saddening and depressing her, detracting from the pleasure of the journey. At the last moment that morning Sister Ambrose had withdrawn from the party to travel, pleading illness, and this had further angered Ida, as she had thought the visit might offer opportunities for the revenge she must surely take.

The journey up to this point had proved uneventful. They had encountered only a few people going in the opposite direction, and there had been no reports of trouble on the road ahead. It was a pleasant day, a watery, early spring sun bringing a little warmth to their faces as they travelled, and a general feeling of exuberance had gradually spread through the group as Chester and its troubles were left behind.

None of her fellow travellers seemed to have heard the distant sound of the horn and the younger nuns chattered excitedly amongst themselves as they walked alongside the cart which carried their older companions.

Ida, however, had heard, and as she led one of the packhorses along the trail her sharp young eyes searched the hillside ahead for the source of the noise. She thought she detected some movement near the brow of a hill in the distance, but, staring almost directly into the sun, she could not be certain. Somehow, though, she knew, was absolutely sure in her mind, that danger threatened.

At the crossroads preparations were almost complete. Morgan and three of his villains were hidden in the undergrowth on either side of the track the nuns were travelling. The fourth was positioned a little further down the track to cut off any would-be escapees. They would not attack before assessing the strength of the approaching party, no chances would be taken, so they lay in their places, silently waiting.

Nearing the same crossroads along the track running south from the village of Kingsley, their approach unseen since the withdrawal of the lookouts for the ambush, were the monks from Norton Priory and one of their number, John of Dutton, had also heard the horn. As one hounded in the past for his "crime", his instincts were honed to a fine edge, and he, like Ida, sensed danger. He tightened his grip on the stout staff he carried and his eyes searched the bushes at each side of the track, looking for clues, seeking to gain any advantage he could.

They were deep into the forest now and the low sun could not penetrate the canopy of branches. The track was appreciably darker and the gloom seemed to affect the mood of the nuns. The chattering had subsided and, apart from occasional whispers, they now walked in near silence. To Ida, used as she had been to woods and forests, it was altogether too quiet, with not even a birdsong to be heard.

As a country dweller, John, too, "felt" the lack of noise. He was certain now that danger was imminent and intimated as much to his brethren. They, too, had become aware of the threat and the tension in the air, and those with weapons came to a state of readiness.

The silence was suddenly shattered by shouts and screams from ahead of them. Morgan's cutthroats had pounced on the nuns' little group with terrifying effect. The two old men in the party, one leading the second packhorse, the other the driver of the cart, were despatched instantly and without mercy, savagely cut down by violent sword thrusts. The Mother Superior and the two old nuns riding on the cart were dragged down and thrown to the ground where they lay sobbing. At the first sign of the attack several of the younger sisters had tried to escape, turning to run into the forest. They were quickly rounded up and returned to the scene of the ambush.

Only Ida had stood her ground. With her back to the bole of a large oak, she faced the outlaws, armed with a broken branch she had snatched up from the ground.

"Aaah, one with spirit at last!" roared Morgan. "Take her, lads, but do not damage her, she'll give us fine sport later."

One of his thugs moved towards Ida, grinning evilly.

"Come by, my little puppy," he sneered, reaching out a filthy hand towards her. A second later he was howling with pain as the branch Ida was wielding smashed into the outstretched arm.

"You little bitch," he screamed, "you'll suffer for that."

Morgan and the others howled with laughter.

"It's you that is suffering, Owen," one cried, and the rest hooted and jeered.

Incensed, Owen rushed forward again, but Ida never flinched. This time her thrust was straight and the jagged end of the broken branch rammed into the face of the charging man. Now, blood was spurting from his head and he reeled back blinded, clutching his face with both hands. For the first time Ida left the base of the tree. Stepping quickly forward she kicked the thug in the groin with all her strength. With an anguished moan he sank to the ground and as he lay there the branch rose and fell again, landing with a sickening crunch on his skull. Now he lay still, blood pouring from his face and ears. He had robbed his last victim.

Save for Ida's laboured breathing and the whimpering of her companions, a silence had settled on the clearing. Now Morgan slowly edged forward, his razor-edged sword advanced before him.

"Morgan will tame you, she-cat, Morgan will draw your claws. Before this day is through you shall rue the day you were born."

His advance was checked by a crashing in the undergrowth to his rear, and through the bushes burst the monks from Norton, at their head John of Dutton. He took in the scene at a glance and, staff whirling, took on the two villains nearest the cart. They fell to the ground stunned and were quickly despatched by his companions following up.

This distraction gave Ida the chance she needed. As Morgan turned to meet this fresh challenge, she again left the shelter of the tree. Again the branch rose and fell, but at the last second some sixth sense warned Morgan and he half turned and ducked, the branch merely catching him a glancing blow on the shoulder.

This gave John his opportunity to strike and he delivered a telling blow to Morgan's back, pushing him towards Ida again. She, in turn, thrust again and he staggered sideways. Another of the monks now joined the fray, running in to try to drag Morgan down. His reward for this effort was a mighty backhanded slash from Morgan's sword which took his head clean from his shoulders, great gouts of blood spurting from the neck as the body fell twitching to the floor.

The sight of blood inspired the Welshman and shocked the others and he went onto the attack, charging at John, sword flailing. John parried desperately but felt the great strength of the brute as the shock of the blows ran through the stout staff into his arms and shoulders. He was backing off now and his companions seemed unable to move, paralysed by the ferocity of Morgan's attack, his terrifying battle screams dulling their senses.

Only Ida seemed capable of action. She snatched up the fallen sword of the thug she had felled and ran towards the bandit leader. As he drove John back his bellowing grew louder, triumph in his voice now as he saw the fear in the young man's eyes. John tripped and fell backwards and the sword was raised for the death-blow. Ida arrived at a run, the sword she held carried like a lance. As Morgan's weapon started its descent, Ida's drove upwards through the ribs beneath his right shoulder, on through his heart and lungs, and out through his chest beneath the left collar-bone. The impetus of her charge carried him over the fallen John to land a few feet away in the mud of the track, the blade of the sword breaking with a sharp crack as he fell, dead before he hit the ground.

"Mighty Morgan, you will tame no more she-cats," she spat at the fallen figure, and, as John lay on the ground he was amazed at the hatred he saw in the young face, the raw animal blood-lust.

In an instant it was gone, and she turned towards him.

"Thank you, brother, we owe you our lives."

"And I mine to you, good sister," he replied.

Their eyes met and a special look passed between them, of respect and admiration, and, too, a mutual understanding that neither was as they outwardly appeared.

Then Ida turned abruptly away, as if regretting the bond they had established by the look. He was mystified and hurt by the sudden change of mood, but put it down to the shock of the attack. After all, it was not every day that a woman killed two men!

During the scuffle the remaining bandit, now heavily outnumbered, and having witnessed the fate of his leader, took to his heels, fleeing deep into the forest. Three of John's group made to follow but he quickly stopped them.

"Let him go. He will not return, but following him into his own domain could bring great danger. Together we will be safe."

The nuns were gathered around the decapitated monk, covering the severed neck with his hood. One of his companions took up the head and placed it next to the body. Nothing could be done for the poor brave man. He had been no match for the brute who had slain him – a man of peace gone now to his reward in Heaven.

Ida unstrapped one of the saddlebags on her packhorse and from amongst her belongings produced her package of medicaments. Several of the nuns had received scrapes and bruises which she treated with one of her salves and bound with bandages. The two old men who had travelled with them from Chester were quite beyond mortal help. The only consolation was that Morgan and three of his henchmen were also dead, and despatched to Hell. From this day forward the forest would be a safer place.

Together, they righted the cart and loaded the bodies of the two old men and the young monk on to it. They would be given a Christian burial when they reached their destination, but Morgan and his men were interred in a shallow grave scratched in the soft loam beneath the trees.

Monks and nuns stood together for a moment in a brief prayer for their attackers as the grave was filled in. Ida stood apart from them, no forgiveness in her heart, her conscience untroubled that two of them had died by her hand.

John of Dutton watched as Ida stood, tall and proud, head unbowed, and thought: " What manner of woman is this?"

As the group moved away from the scene of the attack, Ida brought up the rear and he took up a place alongside her. They walked for a long time in silence before John spoke.

"You fight better than many men I know, " he said.

There was no reply from the girl but she turned her head to look at him and he saw again, in her eyes, that flash of hatred he had seen as she had gutted the bandit.

He tried again. " We are your friends, your brothers, we seek the same truth."

This time he was rewarded with an answer.

"Is any man my friend: do you not all seek the same thing from a woman?" she spat at him.

He reached out to touch her but the expression on her face forbade it and he let his hand drop to his side. For several more minutes they walked on, and John thought of the glance they had exchanged after Morgan's death. There had been admiration then, and need. The same need he himself felt, to talk to someone of a kindred spirit, someone who could understand his regrets, his loss of friends and family and home, because he missed greatly all of these things. Perhaps she, too, had these needs, and missed the things he missed.

He had companions but needed friends, could it be that here was another with those self-same needs? He resolved that in the days ahead he would find out the answer to his question.

Ida, for her part, was wondering if she had, perhaps, been too hasty in her judgement of this man. Her experiences with the opposite sex to date had left her with only suspicion and loathing; the village boys, the men who had raped and killed Anne Bickerton, the thieving little brat in the city, and this latest episode in the forest had done nothing to enamour her to the male sex.

As they walked, she cast a discreet sidelong glance at her companion. He was tall and handsome, his skin tanned and healthy. His gait was that of a country dweller, strong, mile consuming, his eyes staring ahead keen and determined, vigilant, searching. His whole demeanour was foreign to her image of a man of the cloth, and totally at odds with that of the other men she had encountered at first hand. He was courageous and strong: the scuffle back down the track had proved that much. Yes, maybe he could be different, certainly there was something about him that attracted her. He made no further attempt to engage her in conversation, and she was happy to accept the silence, reserving her judgement till she could get to know more about him.

Slowly, the little group continued their journey, coming ever closer to their destination, and, in some cases, their lives' destinies...

Chapter Sixteen

They had established a routine of almost total indifference towards each other's activities. Each did the minimum necessary to maintain the marriage, Ian going off to work each morning and Jane coping with the domestic chores, though neither with any great enthusiasm for what they did. Strangely, though, neither seemed to hold any great grudge against the other. They had settled into a quite amicable state of co-habitation, each having a private obsession with which to occupy the mind.

Jane was in the eighth month of her pregnancy and was now a picture of health, the epitome of near-motherhood. She had accumulated a roomful of "baby things": clothing, cot, baby chair, teddybear, dolls and a sufficiency of toilet requisites to stock a children's home.

All these items she examined and admired, re-arranged on a daily basis and added to on a weekly basis. Had she spent the money on herself which she had spent on the baby, she would have felt guilty, and had Ian realised, he would have hit the roof. As it was, he didn't know and she didn't care. If he could spend every waking leisure moment with his "other woman", as she had come to regard his quest, then to hell with him and the expense!

Ian's research was painstakingly slow, but he read on, absorbed in his latest book, borrowed that weekend from the library. Slowly, a piece at a time, further scraps of information were emerging. He had discovered the tale behind the foundation of the Abbey, the pledge, by Prince Edward, when in fear of drowning on his return from a crusade, to dedicate a great place of worship in thanks for his deliverance. He had read of the construction work undertaken over a period of fifty years, and of the violent storm and gale which, in 1360, had virtually undone, in a few moments, the results of that half century of toil.

He had found details of the subsequent systematic dismantling of the ruins after the Act of Supremacy of 1533, when much of the stone from the original structure had been either removed from the site or re-used for other buildings of the new religious order in the vicinity.

He had learned of how the Abbey and its estate had then passed from owner to owner, for money or for favours rendered, of the blood-letting perpetrated in the name of religion and the law, and of the corruption and greed inherent in the division of the spoils.

Coming right up to modern times, the story had been a sad one, of misuse and neglect, reaching the stage when the lovely old building had lain for years, empty and crumbling, open to the elements, the squatters and the vandals, while the planners and conservationists had argued the toss over what should be done with it.

He was thankful that good sense had finally prevailed and that the building was once again set to play an important role in the local community, both as a leisure facility and in providing some much-needed jobs.

Only rarely, and then vaguely, had he found mention of the Nun's Grave, or, more specifically, the mysterious lady herself. He had seen old photographs of the gravestone in books in the library and a transcription, purported to be from the gravestone, which read,

" The souls of those that die
Are but sunbeams lifted higher."

On the pieces of the monument he had seen, there had been no such inscription and he now wondered if it was on the base section, perhaps badly weathered or overgrown. This evening, he decided, he would take another look before the daylight faded. Just another few pages to the end of the current chapter, that should still leave him with sufficient time to get to the graveside before darkness fell, and be home in time for an early night.

For weeks he had not slept well, for sleep brought vivid dreams of a mysterious nun whose face he never saw, of monks and a magnificent monastery, of cats and graves, of books, babies, blood and death, all a-jumble in his poor, tired brain.

In the event it took a little longer than he had anticipated to finish the chapter and, as an afterthought, he turned back shortly after leaving the house to pick up the small torch they kept in the kitchen drawer. He approached the railings surrounding the plinth in semi-darkness, flashing the torch occasionally to light his way and noticing as he did so that since his last visit the area was considerably tidier. The railings had been given a coat of paint, the moss had been scraped from the old stonework and the grass was shorter and neater. Much improved, he nodded, appreciatively, more like the old days.

"That's strange," he muttered to himself at the thought. "How would I know what it was like in the old days?"

He flicked on the torch and was able to make out some lettering near the base of the plinth where the grass had been recently cut back. The words, weather-beaten though they were, he could make out to be the same ones he had read in the library:

THE SOULS OF THOSE THAT DIE
ARE BUT SUNBEAMS LIFTED HIGHER

He felt a thrill of excitement and pleasure. At last he had made a direct connection between the written and the actual.

As he knelt before the grave, his eyes scanning the wording, he heard a sound like far-off music seeming to come from below the ground between his knees. It was a strange archaic sound and with it, as it rose, came a long drawn-out, heart-rending sigh, so profound, so poignant, that a dreadful feeling of sadness and tragedy almost overwhelmed him.

Suddenly, he became aware of another sound, that of movement behind him, and the small hairs on the back of his neck stood on end and his skin crawled. He froze, holding his breath, unable to move, not daring to turn and a voice said,

"Good evening, sir. Now what would you be doing out here in the dark, then?"

Ian almost fainted with relief, and let out his breath in a long gasp.

Looking up he recognised the face of the night-watchman he had spoken to on previous occasions.

"Oh, it's a bit silly really, but I found something in a book and I

71

just needed to check it out. Sorry I'm being a nuisance, I'll be on my way."

"That's okay, sir, it all helps to pass the night."

Ian got to his feet and turned away, then, as an afterthought, asked the watchman: "Have you ever heard music out here during the night?"

"Music, sir, no, can't say as I have. Mind you I don't come here if I can help it – always feels a bit spooky to me, so I keep away. Goodnight, sir."

The watchman walked away saying to himself: "Must keep an eye on this one, he's a bloody nutter."

For a moment or two longer Ian remained, the light from the torch lighting the gravestone and casting a deep shadow beyond it. Deep within that shadow there was movement and again Ian caught his breath in fear. He laughed nervously as the light reflected in the yellow eyes of a large, jet-black cat, which leapt up onto the plinth.

This sudden appearance broke the spell and Ian turned away from the stone and headed for home. As he walked his mind was in turmoil. What had happened here to create such an atmosphere of grief and misery, he wondered? For that was what he had felt, such sorrow and anguish as he had never before known. And fear, too.

As he entered the house, for the first time in weeks he thought of Jane. She sat at the fireside, as usual knitting, and he thought of the baby, close now, and realised what an idiot he had been, letting this nun take over his life. Thanks to her he was farther away from Jane than he had ever been since they met. He really must make the effort and put it all behind him, at least until the baby was born.

He went to sit beside Jane.

"Hello, darling," he whispered, "what's that you're making?"

"Just a little jumper for baby," she replied, holding out the pattern. "You can't have too many, can you ?"

She smiled at him, that smile he had loved since they were schoolkids, and suddenly it was as if nothing had ever gone wrong. They chatted then for hours about all the things they had neglected for the last few months but mostly about the baby, and Ian, for the first time, felt that the baby was his too, and that Jane needed him to be a part of it all.

That night, for the first time in months, they fell asleep in each other's arms, and for the first time in months Ian's sleep was free from dreams.

Chapter Seventeen

The rest of the journey through the forest had proved uneventful. The road was clearly defined, having been much used over the years for the transport from the quarry and the forest of the very stone and timber from which the Abbey, their destination, had been constructed. So, in less than two hours, the object of their journey came into sight.

For those travellers visiting Vale Royal for the first time, the impression was one of magnificent man-made grandeur, set in an area of outstanding natural beauty.

A long lane, lined with trees of many varieties, led the eye up to the Abbey itself, situated on a rise in the ground, completely dominating the surrounding area. It was a magnificent creation, a monument in itself to the hundreds of craftsmen who had laboured for half a century and more on its fabric. Towering spires reached beseeching fingers to the heavens and great stone arches yawned a welcome, inviting the weary pilgrims to enter. Inside, its huge windows depicted scenes from the scriptures, sculpted in lead and translucent glass in myriad colours.

As the various bands of travellers reached their journey's end, many sank to their knees, in thanks for safe deliverance but also in awe at the sight which greeted them. In Ida's party many were moved to tears at the splendour and majesty of this House of God.

Even Ida, though not yet fully integrated, and largely lacking in religious piety, was greatly impressed by the spectacle. John was likewise affected as he stood at her side.

As a country dweller his practised eye took in the fields and woods surrounding the structure, assessing the potential for agriculture and for hunting: so much inherent wealth. Through a gap in the trees to the left of the building he could see that the land dropped away to a river, no doubt rich in fish and waterfowl, in the valley below.

The monks who emerged to greet them looked hearty, well-fed fellows, clear of complexion and eye, no doubt living off the fat of the land, which, in this particular instance, seemed fat indeed.

Helping with the baggage, they led the various parties to the quarters allocated to them. The nuns from St. Mary's were housed in an annexe to the main building tucked into a clearing in the woodland near to the east wing. The monks were escorted into the Abbey itself, taking their places amongst the resident brothers as directed, where they proceeded to tell of their journey and its pitfalls.

By noon the following day it was reckoned that all establishments sending visitors had been accounted for, and in a simple ceremony those poor souls who had succumbed on the journey were laid to rest, the young monk from the Norton party being buried in the graveyard at the side of the Abbey, the others in the churchyard in the little village of Whitegate, nearby.

Instructions then began as to what form the celebrations would take. Prayers were to occupy much of each day, services to be held four times daily, and this was to be the case for the whole of their stay, culminating on the twenty-first day of the month in a great feast of celebration dedicated to their founder, Saint Benedict.

Of all the gathered throng, the person to whom this probably meant the least was Ida. For the sake of appearances she showed her face at the morning services that first day, but, with so many present, mostly deeply involved in their own devotions, she quickly realised that her absence would not readily be noticed.

To Ida, this was an opportunity to get back to the world she loved, to the trees and plants she knew so well. A chance too, perhaps, to gather some of the herbs she needed to replenish her stocks of potions and balms. Though this was not the ideal season of the year for this, there might be some things she could find and the searching itself would bring her great pleasure.

That night sleep came quickly as the rigours of the day took their toll, and, as she drifted away, Ida's thoughts were on the morrow, the slaughter of the day erased from her mind.

The next day broke fine, though cold, and she slipped quietly away from her quarters and followed a path through the wood in the direction of the river, a small bag containing a little food across her shoulder. Spring was on its way and the green shoots of new life were prominent everywhere. It needed little in the way of imagination to picture the place as it would be in the summer when all would be in full bloom, or in the autumn when nature would paint the landscape in its superb range of yellows, reds and browns.

From a rookery in the branches of a great ash came the loud, harsh cawings of the nest builders, preparing the crude rafts of twigs which would receive the eggs. She sat a while on a fallen tree trunk, watching the wheeling and diving of the ugly black birds, laughing at their quarrels and clumsiness.

Moving further on she came to a small clearing which opened out onto the bank of the river. At the river's edge was a small boathouse, a little rowing boat moored alongside it. She climbed into the boat and sat, rocking gently, gazing up and down stream in turn, taking in the activities of the coots and moorhens as they, too, went about their construction work. She spotted a large grey and white heron, in motionless, predatory pose at the water's edge, its great pointed yellow beak ready to spear any unwitting creature which might come within range.

A few sheep and cattle grazed the meadow of the flood plain on the opposite bank and the lone figure of one of the lay brothers wandered listlessly around them, starting to round them up for the drive back to the abbey for the morning milking. Ida leaned back to lie across the thwarts of the boat. It would not, perhaps, be wise to be seen by anyone lest questions were asked. She did not think she would be missed but the fewer people aware of her wanderings the better.

From the cover of the boat she watched as the monk across the river rounded up his charges and drove them away downstream to where she assumed there must be a bridge. Tomorrow, she thought, she would go that way to find out; meanwhile she was content just to sit in this lovely spot and observe, and, as she did so, she instinctively became aware that she, too, was being watched.

John had seen her furtive departure from the chapel after the early prayer service and smiled to himself. This girl and he were obviously of a mind, for he, too, had no intentions of spending the whole of his visit in devotions and meditation. It was clear to him that Ida did not belong, any more than he did, to the Order from personal choice. What circumstances, he wondered, had brought her to the convent? Maybe over the next few days he could find out.

He had trailed her through the wood, stopping when she stopped, enjoying her obvious pleasure as she drank in the delights of her surroundings. Now, using all the skills he had learned as a youth stalking some item of game for the pot, he closed on the girl in the boat, moving silently from tree to tree, coming ever closer to where she lay, keeping the boathouse between them for cover.

Having reached the building, it was his intention to make some little noise to alert her to his presence, but his plan was doomed to failure. As he stuck his head round the corner for a final glance he was rewarded with a resounding smack in the face, then, before he could recover, he was snatched forward, off balance, and dumped unceremoniously into the river alongside the now empty boat. He came up gasping, the cold water snatching his breath away, to see Ida grinning down on him.

"Cool down, good brother," she mocked, "the blood runs too hot within you."

"I planned you no hurt," he spluttered as he dragged himself up the bank. "I need a friend to talk to, someone who feels as I do. I think you could be that friend if you would but give me the chance to talk to you."

He stood erect, water streaming from his sodden habit, hair plastered to his head, teeth chattering from the cold. He turned away from Ida and entered the boathouse. For a few moments she hesitated, then followed him inside. He had found some rags and a rough work smock hung on a peg on the wall. He stood naked, his back to the door, towelling himself with the rags.

As he dried himself Ida watched the lines of muscle working in his shoulders and back. She took in the slimness of his waist and hips, the firmness of his buttocks and legs, and in that moment she knew that she wanted him.

She had known, she supposed, since the fight in the forest that he was different. His dark good looks, his manner, his voice, the honesty of his eyes, had all combined to tell her that this man was one she could trust. In a way he was like the old priest from the village, the only other man in her short life she had had much to do with.

He became aware of her presence and snatched the smock from the peg, embarrassed by his nakedness, trying to cover himself and blushing as she laughed gently.

"So, then, good brother monk, talk to me, convince me that you are my friend..."

She reached out and snatched the smock from his hand, leaving him as naked as the day he was born. His attraction to her was conspicuously apparent and she gazed down on him, her own desire now manifesting itself in the damp warmth spreading between her legs. She slipped out of her cloak, letting it fall to the floor, then wriggled free of her habit. She stood before him now wearing nothing but the thin shift which was her only undergarment. Through the flimsy material he could see the outline of her splendid breasts, her nipples fully erect from cold and desire.

They came together in an embrace that said far more than any words, a long kiss, gentle at first, then evermore hungry. Without a word they sank to the floor. Oblivious to the cold and their crude surroundings they made love, and only then, during the act, did the words begin to flow, unfettered by suspicion or embarrassment. Between times they related, each to the other, something of their young lives and the traumas they had suffered, wallowing in mutual pity and giving comfort in that most natural of ways, with their bodies.

Afterwards they ate the bread and meat she had brought, wolfing it down, made hungry by their efforts. Then they talked for hours, talk interspersed with further bouts of lovemaking, on and on until the daylight began to fade, huddled together beneath Ida's clothes, until the boathouse became too cold for them to bear

78

it any longer. They dressed then, John donning his still wet habit, and made their way back through the woods to the Abbey. They embraced once more at the edge of the wood, clinging to each other passionately, then split up and made their way back to their separate quarters.

Later that night lying in her cot, Ida relived the ardour of the day just gone. John's caresses had been tender yet unpracticed, she thought, his actions nervous and unsure. They had guided and helped each other through the love-making, two enthusiastic newcomers to the art. Tomorrow, she told herself, it would be better; each day would bring greater pleasures as their knowledge grew.

John, too, lay sleepless that night. This had been the first time his passions had gone beyond the stage of self-gratification, and a fresh stirring came to his loins as his thoughts went through the events of the day. His conscience was untroubled. The girl had known what she wanted as much as he had, and had shown no reluctance or regret during or after their first coupling. Rather, she had approached it with great fervour, urging him on long after he was spent, instigating much of the subsequent ardour of the day. Tomorrow, he decided, he must be better prepared, the experience of today must not go to waste.

As each day of their stay went by their love grew, their expression of it deepened and expanded, bringing them both to new heights of pleasure. They roamed the woods and riverbanks, seeking new love-nests away from prying eyes, taking with them blankets and food, hidden beneath their garb, spending hours together. They talked much of the past yet each seemed reluctant to raise the subject of the future.

The shadow of the Church hung over them, their commitment to it, though not yet pledged, certainly implied, holding them back from a deeper commitment to each other. Each knew that at the end of the current celebrations they must return to the life they had chosen, for long enough, at the very least, to sever any ties cleanly, so that any future they might plan together would be uncluttered by recriminations from the Order.

On the penultimate day of the festival they lay together on a hilltop a mile or so north of the Abbey, overlooking the water-mill and the river running down to the boathouse and the Abbey beyond.

From this vantage point they had a splendid view of the whole area, and, once again they marvelled at the scene. They had made love for what they knew must be the last time till they might meet again, and when that would be they could not be sure. Now they made their uncertain plans for the future.

"When I get back to Norton I will make my peace with the Prior," John said. "Then in a few weeks I will come to Chester for you. We can find a home somewhere, though I have nothing by way of wealth or belongings."

"I need nothing but you," whispered Ida. "When you come I shall be ready. There is something I have vowed to do before I leave; when it is done there will be nothing to hold me there."

Her expression as she said this was grim, her eyes set on some distant object, shutting John out of her presence. For fully a minute she stared, then nodded her head once,

"Yes, this I must do, then I am yours, for ever if you want me."

"For ever it shall be," John replied, "and some day, I promise, we shall return to this place, to live again our love of these few days."

They lay together then, in silence, and a chill, not just of the weather, came over them, where there should have been a glow of warmth.

Chapter Eighteen

The birth had gone very badly and for three days Jane had lain in a semi-coma in the post-natal care unit at the hospital, whilst the baby, a boy, was in an incubator in the special baby unit. Both were fairly poorly and Ian was devastated, flitting from bedside to incubator in despair, praying that these two people, who he loved more than anything in the world, would not be taken from him now. The medical staff were not over-concerned, having seem all these things before, but to Ian, coming on top of the affairs of the last few months, it seemed like a form of judgement, a punishment for his selfish behaviour.

Ian's company had been very understanding and granted him leave from his job, though some of his work he was managing to do from home, even though he found it difficult to concentrate his thoughts for long on the matter in hand. During the lonely hours spent at home between hospital visits, in spite of himself he found his thoughts once again drawn back to his search for the truth behind the nun's story.

He had once more taken to walking, during the late evenings, in the vicinity of the grave. It was on one of these occasions that he adopted the cat, or, at least, the cat adopted him.

As he approached the plinth one evening, he found a huge, jet-black cat, the same one, he thought, he had come across before, curled up asleep on the first step of the plinth, immediately above the inscription. It awoke as he arrived, stretched, long and sinuously, as only cats can, and commenced to groom, showing no fear at his approach.

"Hello, my beauty, where have you come from?" Ian asked, reaching down to stroke the animal.

It stood up, legs straight, back arched, tail erect and quivering, a deep throaty purr confirming its pleasure as it pushed its great ebony head into his hand, marking him with its scent glands. This show of affection deeply affected Ian, bringing tears to his eyes and a fond smile to his face as his thoughts went immediately out to Jane and his son.

Jane had always loved cats and it was only his own insistence that had prevented her having one when they moved into the new house. They were very tying, he had argued; but they're so gorgeous, she had replied, especially lovely fluffy little kittens.

"Well, you're no fluffy little kitten, are you?" he addressed the cat, "but I bet she'd like you just the same."

The cat had by now jumped from the plinth to the ground and was rubbing itself against his legs, purring and miaowing for all it was worth. He bent and picked it up, feeling, as he did so, the raw power of the sinewy body. The cat was in an ecstasy of delight and rubbed against his face and neck, purring the while.

The watchman suddenly appeared, emerging from the rear of the main building, whistling as he walked towards them.

"Good evening again, sir," he called to Ian, at the same time thinking: "Oh God, he's here again, and this time he's got a bloody great panther with him!"

At his voice the cat squirmed from Ian's grasp and leapt to the ground, running off a few yards then turning to face the newcomer. The purr had gone now and the huge yellow eyes glared unblinkingly at the man.

"Where did you find that brute?" the watchman asked.

"I didn't," said Ian. "He was here when I arrived. I was wondering who he belonged to."

"Well, he ain't mine, I've never set eyes on him before," said the watchman. "Big bugger isn't he?"

The "big bugger" never took its eyes off the man's face and he felt a little thrill of fear at the stare. He bent and picked up a stick which he swished at the animal. At his movement the cat sank to its belly, baring huge white fangs, a deep growl rumbling in its throat, the transformation, from cuddly pet to wild beast, completed in a second. The watchman threw the stick but the cat avoided it with ridiculous ease, bounding to one side, its eyes still fixed on the man.

"Bloody vicious sod," he grumbled, then, abashed, walked away. "Goodnight, sir, watch yourself with that bloody thing."

82

Ian grinned at the retreating back then turned back to the cat.

"Well, big bugger, you've certainly made a good impression there. You'll have to watch out for him in the future."

He could have sworn that the cat grinned back. As he turned for home the cat followed, or rather led, him, padding along the path a couple of yards ahead, turning now and again to make sure Ian was following. As Ian reached the house and opened the back door, it pushed past him and trotted into the lounge where it promptly curled up before the remnants of the fire, and in a few moments settled into a deep sleep, a throaty, growling purr signifying its contentment at the situation.

"Cheeky bugger, too!" Ian said, but made no move to evict the incumbent.

"Well, Jane, looks like you've got your own way after all."

Ian's prayers for his wife and child were soon to be answered, for, with each day that passed, both Jane and her baby became stronger as all the skills of the doctors and nursing staff paid off.

Each evening Ian would sit near the fire and update the cat on the progress of Jane and the baby, and the cat seemed to understand his every word, its eyes following his every gesture.

Another week passed slowly and then they were allowed home. He had kept the news of the cat's arrival from Jane, meaning it to be a surprise on her homecoming. As the car turned into the drive and stopped, the surprise turned into a shock. No sooner had the vehicle stopped moving than the cat bounded onto the bonnet, landing right in front of Jane and peering through the windscreen directly into her face. She let out a scream of fright as the huge yellow eyes met hers. Ian laughed.

"Jane, meet Big Bugger," he said. "Big Bugger, this is Jane."

After the initial shock Jane was thrilled as Ian explained the circumstances of the cat's arrival.

"So he came home with me, and here he has stayed since. Nobody's claimed him so I think we've got him for good."

"Or for as long as he decides to stay," Jane replied. "You don't know cats like I do, they very much do their own thing. But he's a lovely boy, and I'm thrilled to bits. You'll have to look after him though, I'll have enough to do with this little fellow."

She unstrapped the carry-cot from the rear seat and lifted it out, smiling down at her son who lay asleep there. The cat, as though not to be outdone, sprang with casual ease from bonnet to car roof, from which vantage point he could also see into the cot. A loud miaow signified his approval of what he saw and Jane laughed with pleasure at the sound.

The family moved into the house.

Chapter Nineteen

The morning after the great festival of celebration was one of intense activity as the various parties of visitors made their preparations for leaving. Ida and John's groups left at the same time, planning to travel together as far as the crossroads in the forest for mutual protection, along with a few of the monks from Vale Royal who were going on a reciprocal visit to St. Werburgh's Abbey in Chester.

Ida and John walked together, bringing up the rear. They had little to say that had not already been said, but once again reassured each other that the promises they had made and their plans for a future together had been sincere. As they neared the place where their paths were to part they lagged a little further behind the main party and stopped. John took Ida into his arms and gently kissed her.

"I shall come for you, my darling, this I swear. No matter how long, never forget that I love you. Wait for me," he whispered.

Ida returned his kisses passionately, crushing herself to his chest. She raised her head to look at his face and he saw the tears well up in her eyes.

"I will wait," she answered. "If it takes for ever, I will be there when you come."

With that, she turned away from him and ran to catch up with the main party.

He watched her go, the pain in his heart mingled with the joy of what he had found during the preceding fortnight. His last sight was of her tall, young figure disappearing round a slight bend in the road. She never looked back. For a moment he was tempted to run after her, take her now, and to hell with the consequences, but then he thought better of it. They had made their plans, and they would stick to them; the delight of their reunion would be all the sweeter.

* * * * *

During the fight at the crossroads, the only survivor of Morgan's band, Rees Ap-Thomas, had run for his life. When the sounds of pursuit had stopped, he had circled round and crept back to the scene from another direction, then watched from cover as his companions' bodies were buried. The last to be dragged into the shallow grave had been that of his young brother, David, the one who had rushed Ida at the tree. Rees had watched as the earth covered the gore-smeared young face, hearing again, in his mind, the grating crack as Ida had crushed his skull and in that moment he had sworn vengeance on his brother's executioner. But Rees was a coward at heart, with no stomach for a face-to-face battle. His was the bravery of the ambush, the knife in the back; the weaker the victim, the greater he relished the task.

Now, from his hiding place near the crossroads, he watched as the returning body of travellers divided. He saw the young nun run to catch up with her party and recognised her as the one who had killed Morgan and his brother. Well, Morgan had had it coming to him, he thought. He had always had the lion's share of the spoils, now he had paid the full price and he, Rees, had everything. But his poor dead brother had nothing save a hole in the ground in this accursed place. Back at the hideout he had ransacked the others' belongings and now considered himself a rich man. But family duty was to avenge his brother, so he set off to trail the weaker party, that of the nuns, on the road to Chester. He had waited over two weeks already for his revenge, a little more time did not matter.

It was late in the day when they arrived, travel-stained and weary, at St. Mary's. The monks who had travelled with them made their farewells and headed for the Abbey of St. Werburgh, and Rees, who had trailed them all the way unseen, watched now from his vantage point behind a stone column as the nuns filed into the convent. It took him only a few minutes to find a place nearby in which to stay, a filthy, cramped room above a tavern near the castle, from where he could see the convent.

Over the next few days he watched and followed as the little groups of nuns took up again their work of charity, visiting and feeding the sick and poor around the city. He saw few opportunities for carrying out his plan of murder in safety, and he knew from bitter experience that his target was not a soft one. There was no margin for error, this one was dangerous, and he might not get a second chance, his brother had not. So, he watched and waited, spied and schemed, determined to have his revenge, even though it might be months in coming.

When the tale of Ida's bravery was recounted to the sisters who had not made the journey, she was looked on with something akin to reverence, and the story soon spread outside the convent, so that everywhere she went she was pointed out as the saviour of the party. This adulation served to fuel still further the malignant hatred of Sister Ambrose. She, too, was still set on avenging her dead lover, but also very wary of Ida's ability to strike first. So, she watched and waited, spied and schemed.

Chapter Twenty

The nausea had been with her for a few weeks, but only in the mornings shortly after she rose, confirming what she had instinctively known, that she was carrying John's child. That had since passed and with each week that went by she had grown.

He had said he would come in a few weeks, but over six months had passed without word. She sensed that something was wrong. Ida was confident he would not betray her trust. It had been so good, so sincere: he would come, she knew he would, and when he came he would be thrilled at this news.

She concentrated her thoughts on him, summoning up a picture of his clean, handsome features.

"Where are you, my love," she whispered, "why do you not come to me?"

Twenty or so miles away, where he lay on his sick-bed, John stirred into wakefulness. As he moved, the pain knifed through his leg and he groaned. He pushed himself up onto his elbows, trying to take the weight off the damaged limb, to ease the agony.

For over three months he had been confined to his room, helpless, cursing the cruel trick of fate which now bound him to this bed of pain.

The accident had occurred while they had been loading a cart in the courtyard. John had been standing on the back when the horse had lurched suddenly forward, jerking the cart from beneath him. He had fallen heavily onto the cobbled yard, the sack of meal across his broad shoulders adding to the impact as he landed. The break had not been a clean one and within days infection had set in. His fellow brothers had done all they could to help, setting and dressing the shattered limb, but the fever had run its full course, taking him to the very brink of death.

In his lucid moments his thoughts had turned to Ida, her lovely face floated before him and the strength of his love for her helped him through the crisis, his will to live strengthened by his need to go to her. He knew though, that it would be weeks still before he would be fit to make the journey, and his frustration at this help-lessness increased daily. His inability to communicate with Ida also worried him, he had made a vow to her and he was a man of his word. He would go to her, if only she could know why he had not.

Somehow he must try to send the message to her, reassure her, make her understand that he would come, just as soon as his damaged body would allow him. If only she could hear his words, understand his torment, then she would know and wait.

He closed his eyes and pictured again her face, then, concen-trating all his mind on the vision, he murmured over and over again: "I will come, my love, please wait, please wait, please wait..."

The effort tired him greatly, but as he drifted back into sleep he thought he heard her voice saying: "I will wait, if it takes for ever, I will be yours....".

In the convent Ida felt better, assured that her thoughts had reached John and that he would come to her when he could. She sensed that something was wrong but over-riding that came an inner conviction that all would eventually be well.

She gathered up her things and moved into the hallway where the nuns gathered before setting out into the city on their work. She was today to work in a party of four, covering one of the more desperate areas of the city, near the wharves where the river craft loaded and discharged their cargoes.

Chester had been a busy little port since the time of the Roman occupation, and a flourishing trade was carried on between the towns and villages of the countryside and those of the coast and further afield.

The area round the dock was one of poor housing, built in the shadow of the great walls and liberally endowed with taverns, gaming houses and brothels. It was home to the scum of the city and Rees had accordingly slotted in perfectly.

Each day from his room near the castle he had wandered down into the dock area where he ate, drank, or availed himself of one of the pox-ridden harlots as the need took him, and all the while keeping an eye open for any opportunity of gain.

Yes, he fitted very well into his filthy surroundings. Each night he roamed the streets and alleys, robbing, often for merely a few coins, lonely old women or helpless beggars.

On one occasion he callously slit the throat of an unwary merchant he had trailed from a tavern to the door of his home, relieving him of the fat purse he carried and the gold it contained. On another he battered to death a blind beggar for the few coppers in his begging-bowl, afterwards slipping away, unseen, into the darkness.

As the weeks had passed his store of loot had become considerable and he was ready now to leave the city before things became too hot for him. As yet his crimes had gone undetected, but his luck would not hold for ever. The time had come for him to fulfil his vow: the girl must die before he left.

Each day he had watched for Ida leaving the convent, trying to establish her pattern of movement. Since no set pattern had emerged he had become increasingly frustrated as no chance arose to take his revenge.

Neither were the nuns seen out much after darkness fell, a further obstacle to his designs, as that was when he did his best work. This day he saw her leave, easily distinguishable to him now, her tall straight figure standing out amongst her companions. He followed at a discreet distance, then stopped and watched as they paused near an old beggar who sat at the corner of an alley. Ida knelt at his side, breaking off a piece of bread from the loaf she carried, pressing it into the filthy, outstretched hand.

Then Rees noticed an amazing thing. One of the older nuns stood back from the scene, behind Ida, and the expression on her face excited him. It exuded a degree of hatred and malice which warranted no place in the habit she chose to wear. Never had he seen, in man nor woman, such malevolence as he now saw, and he knew, without any shadow of doubt, that he had found an ally to his evil cause. This woman's hatred of the girl was plain to see, greater possibly than his own.

The group of nuns moved on, stopping now and then to dispense food or medicine, a kindly word, anything to help alleviate the suffering of the impoverished wretches who thronged the waterfront.

Always at the fore was Ida, her presence overshadowing the others. It was to her that the poor turned first and her ready smile and encouraging words helped in some small way to brighten their day. At each stop Rees watched, his attention focussed now not on Ida but on Sister Ambrose. His first impression was confirmed and strengthened with each halt. The more attention and gratitude Ida received, the more apparent became the hate the other woman carried for her.

Ida and two of her companions had now moved into one of the squalid alleyways which ran at right angles to the wharf into the labyrinth of stinking hovels which formed the living quarters of the dock workers and attendant low-life. Rees saw that the older nun hung back, making no attempt to follow them. He sidled up to her, noting the hard lines of her face, the almost masculine set of the jaw, and, over-riding all, the inherent malice in the eyes.

"This is good work you do, Sister," he wheedled ingratiatingly. "I know the Lord will reward you all for your kindness to us."

She stared at him, cold hard eyes boring into his brain, hate there for all to see. Her answer was merely lip-service.

"We serve Our Christ, it is our duty."

"The young one, how is she called?" he asked, and was rewarded by the sudden flash of anger which flared in the eyes.

"She is named Ida," came the reply, "and she is not truly of the Order, but a waif we took in who has greatly honoured us by her presence."

Again, the bitterness, the sarcasm of the reply, confirmed his suspicions.

"But she is so well loved by the people," he insisted. "I have seen how they flock to greet her."

"Aye, like the filthy cattle they are," she growled. "Now begone you blaggard, follow her like the rest."

"I have followed her these many months past, Sister," he said, "and I love her not. I weary now of the chase. My home is far away and I would go there. But first there is a task I must perform, a vow I must fulfil. "

Sister Ambrose's face registered her surprise, and a flicker of interest showed in her eyes.

"What lies are these, rogue?" she asked.

"Rogue I may be, Sister" he replied, "but I tell you true. Since the death of my kinsman and friends in the forest, I have followed this woman."

A gleam of understanding showed in the nun's face. She had heard of Ida's heroics in the forest, of the men she had killed during the fight. Four of the five attackers had died, only one had escaped, and of him nothing further had been heard. She had become sick of hearing the tale, of yet another instance of Ida's success.

"You were in the forest," she asked, "the one who got away?"

He nodded, poised now to take flight, gambling on her reaction.

"I got away, my brother did not. He lies in the forest, far from his home and family, buried not in his native soil. I swore revenge on this woman, I cannot return home till I have taken it."

"Why do you tell me these things," asked Sister Ambrose. "How do you know I will not call the Sheriff's men to take you?"

"I am in your hands," he replied, "call them if you must."

He knew immediately that his gamble had paid off. She did nothing, smiled grimly at him and said,

"Meet me tonight near the old bridge, at nightfall."

Later that night they met as arranged. They discussed their mutual hatred of the girl, Ida, and agreed an alliance to carry out their plans.

From that moment Ida's fate was sealed, her days numbered. They parted having made arrangements to meet again the following week, bearing a common bond between them, their abomination of Ida and a lust for revenge.

Over the months Ida had naturally grown bigger, her pregnancy, now increasingly obvious as she had undressed to bathe or sleep, hidden from her companions only by the folds of her habit and the privacy of her cell. Since the death of Sister Catherine she had struck up no new friendships within the Sisterhood and the disposal of Sister Martine had effectively curtailed the unwanted attentions of Sister Ambrose. Though surrounded by other women and working daily with them and the general public, Ida was essentially alone, and lonely.

Each evening in her cell she would strip off her clothes and sit naked on her bed, stroking the swelling that was the child growing within her, talking to it, her thoughts on John, willing him to come to her and take her away from this place.

But still he did not come, and she knew now that she could not hide her condition from the others for very much longer. Soon she must decide whether to make a full confession to the Mother Superior and throw herself on her mercy, or quit the convent and go to find her loved one.

Already the efforts of her tasks were starting to become too much for her and it could not be long before her secret was discovered.

Chapter Twenty-One

At last John was making some progress. The leg was still causing him a great deal of pain and he realised he would walk for the rest of his life with a limp, but at least he was able to walk, aided by sticks, true, but walk nevertheless.

Time now was of the essence. Over eight months had gone by since they had parted at Vale Royal and he could imagine the doubts which must have raged longtime in the thoughts of Ida.

Each day he had fumed and fretted at his inability to contact her, to reassure her. Now his every effort was spent in building up his strength for the long journey to Chester. Their establishment was not a rich one. They owned no horses or mules and he knew, therefore, that to reach Chester he must walk. At first he was able to cover only short distances, in and around the priory, but gradually his stamina improved.

Day after day he walked, each day a little further, a little longer, the pain never leaving him, but determination driving him on, until he was spending three or four hours a day walking non-stop. At last he considered himself ready and set himself a target. On the first day of the following week he would set off, early in the morning, and by walking all day should, God willing, reach her before darkness fell.

* * * * *

Rees and Sister Ambrose had also set themselves a target, and a day. If their evil plan came to fruition, then Ida had less than twenty-four hours to live. The scene was set, the method of execution was to be horrible, the living death of entombment. They had made their preparations well.

During his nefarious wanderings about the city, in a derelict part of the old Roman castle, down in the cellar area, Rees had discovered a small cell-like room, barely eight feet square and six high. An old store room or such, entered by a tiny doorway, it would provide an ideal prison for one person, and that person was to be Ida. Sister Ambrose had provided Rees with the information on Ida's movements for the following day. They knew that she would be working around the dock area and that her homeward journey in the dusk would take her close to their chosen place of ambush. If they could catch her for just a few minutes alone, she would not be allowed to make it back to the convent.

The pain had come as she lifted the old woman from the floor on to the filthy heap of rags which served as a bed. Ida gasped at the stab of agony and clasped her hands to her stomach, a wave of nausea sweeping over her. In a minute it had passed, but Ida knew that this was a warning, her time was very near. She consoled herself with the fact that this was her final call of what had been a wearying day. She left the hovel where the old woman lived and began to make her way back to the convent, wishing that she had stayed with the others.

She knew now that it was too late to do anything other than go to the Mother Superior and beg her forgiveness and indulgence. Surely she would not be refused in her hour of need, and she was determined, even if disgrace and expulsion were to follow the birth, that she would never allow them to take her baby from her. It was hers and John's alone. After the birth, when she was fully recovered, she would go to Norton Priory find her lover.

If he, for some reason, could not come to her, then she must go to him, take him his child.

With her mind full of these concerns she did not see the blow that felled her: her last conscious thought as she slumped to the ground was for her baby.

Roughly and hurriedly, they dragged her down the worn old steps and bundled her in through the tiny aperture, Rees pulling the unconscious body by the hair, Sister Ambrose kicking and kneeing from the rear. Sister Ambrose contrived to light a small tallow candle she had brought with her, then set it on an outcrop of rock. Together they sat, bound by a mutual thread of hatred for the girl, waiting like two vultures, until consciousness began to return.

Ambrose leaned forward as Ida's eyes blinked open, and the girl groaned in pain and despair as she realised who her assailant was. She looked into the crazed, evil eyes and saw Death beckoning. A second face appeared and she moaned.

"Who...?"

"A friend from the forest," he sniggered, "the forest where my brother lies buried, you bitch!"

He smashed his fist into her face and she felt the teeth crack in her jaw, tasted the salt blood in her mouth.

"Leave her for me, Welshman," spat Sister Ambrose. "I will have pleasure from her before we bid her farewell. It's been a long time."

She reached down and tore Ida's habit away and ripped at the shift she wore beneath, till the girl was almost naked.

"If it's pleasure you're having, well, so am I," snarled Rees, pushing her away. "The bitch shall serve us both!"

Ida rolled agonisingly away from them onto her stomach, dragging the shreds of her shift around her, desperately trying to hide and protect her unborn child but they hauled her back and in doing so recognised her condition. Rather than stirring in them any sense of mercy or compassion, the sight of the bloated abdomen and swollen, milk-laden breasts excited them still further. For the next twenty minutes or so they each indulged in sexual acts of the most perverse and degrading nature they could dream up against the helpless girl, each egging the other on with word and deed to the very depths of depravity.

After several moments of this torment Ida passed out, mercifully oblivious to much that occurred, and continued to occur, long after she had sunk into unconsciousness.

They left her where she lay, beaten and abused, taking with them the candle. It took only a few moments to cover the doorway, rolling against it the large slab of rock and filling in the spaces with the smaller rocks and rubble that Rees had placed in readiness, till not a gap could be seen.

It was the pain that woke her, a deep searing agony that tore at her insides, forcing a dry-throated moan from her lips. As the convulsion passed the pain eased and she lay back, gasping, wet with sweat and shuddering with shock and cold.

Not a glimmer of light showed in her prison and she began to crawl around in the blackness, feeling for a way out. It took only a few moments for her to discover that she was trapped, and, with the realisation came the fear. She began to shout and scream, beating frantically at the rough stone walls with her fists, scratching till her nails were torn and her fingers bloodied.

The second contraction came as she screamed and the pain stabbed through her abdomen again, turning the scream into an animal-like howl, doubling her up with its intensity. Once more it passed, replaced by a dull ache, only to return again and again as the hours slipped by.

Closer and closer together now, the contractions racked her body, till the moment finally arrived when she thought she was being literally torn apart as the birth took place.

Instinctively she reached for the slimy mass between her legs and drew the child to her face, wiping and licking away the unseen blood and mucus, feeling the head, raising the tiny mouth to her own and breathing gently into it. The baby stirred and cried and she wept with relief. She bit through and tied the cord which bonded the child to her, then, with trembling hands, wrapped it in the ragged remains of her clothing, hugging it to her breast where its ready mouth suckled hungrily at her nipple. Her hands explored the tiny body, discovering that it was a boy, and she wept in despair as her thoughts turned to her lover so far away.

Why, in her hour of greatest need, had he abandoned her?

Chapter Twenty-Two

The journey had taken all day. As John arrived in the city darkness was falling, but, as he approached, he could make out the great edifice which could only be the Abbey Cathedral of St.Werburgh, towering above the surrounding buildings.

His enquiries eventually led him to the main entrance to the Abbey. He reached the postern gate in a state of advanced exhaustion, his damaged leg paining him dreadfully, his feet blistered and bleeding within his boots. The monk who opened the gate at his knocking caught him as he staggered and almost fell. John told him of his journey from Norton and asked for shelter for the night and without hesitation this was granted him. Despite his weariness he slept little that night, his mind now alive with the fact that he was so near to his beloved Ida. She would understand, he knew, and soon everything would be as they had vowed.

Next morning, his leg and feet bathed and freshly dressed, he made his way out into the city streets. Though regretting the deception, he had thought it politic not to mention his destination to his fellows at St. Werburgh's, choosing instead to make his enquiries on the streets.

Luck was with him and only the second person he spoke to was able to direct him to St. Mary's. A few minutes laboured walking brought him to the door of that establishment. As he rang the bell at the door his thoughts were a clutter of excitement, nervousness, apprehension even.

Supposing she had changed her mind, not waited? What if she should not accept his explanation? Would she still want him now that he was partially crippled with this twisted leg? These and other emotions ran through his head as the judas window in the door opened and a nun's face appeared.

"Good day to you, Sister," he ventured nervously, disappointed that Ida's had not been the first face he should see.

"And to you, Brother," came the reply. "What is your business at our house?".

"I seek a meeting with one of your companions who I met during the visit to the Abbey at Vale Royal. Her name is Ida, a novice of your house. Pray take her a message, tell her that John of Dutton visits your city and would see her again."

The nun peered closer at him. She had been in the party who had made the journey and now recalled the brave young man who had helped to save them from the villains in the forest, though she thought him much changed, the pain apparent in his face. The judas closed and the main door opened, allowing him into the courtyard.

"Wait here," she said. "I will bring someone to see you."

She disappeared into the building and John stood looking round. It was a quiet, peaceful spot, a low murmur of voices, barely reaching his ears, issued from within the convent, other than that there was silence.

The door in the building opened and from it emerged the figure of an old nun who John remembered from their previous meeting to be the Mother Superior. He tried to kneel as she approached, but his leg would not allow it and he bowed his head instead.

She saw the lines of pain and illness etched in the young face and smiled in compassion. She knew why this young man had suffered so much to come to this house, and the knowledge gave her pleasure. Though old, she was far from being senile. Her eyes and mind were sharp and Ida's activities and absences during their trip to Vale Royal had not gone wholly unnoticed.

Over the years she had known many young girls, full of good intent, come to the convent. She had seen some stay and some leave. Since their return from Vale Royal she had read the signs in Ida's behaviour, recognised the change in her, suspected the cause. The old lady had always been very close to poor Sister Catherine, they had joined the Order at about the same time, and she knew of the affection Catherine and Ida had felt for each other. She realised that it would only be a matter of time before Ida left them. That she was not cut out to be a true daughter of the Church had been apparent from the start. True, she had become a novice, but the old Abbess had never considered it likely that Ida would become a fully-fledged member of the Order.

This young man, she knew, had come to take Ida away, and though she would be sorry to see the girl leave, she knew she could not stand in her way and would release her from her vows.

The young monk spoke: "Holy Mother, forgive this intrusion on your privacy. I am John of Dutton and a lay brother from the Priory at Norton. I have travelled these many miles to fulfil a vow I made to one of your Sisters, whom I met on the journey to Vale Royal. I beg your indulgence in this matter and ask your permission to speak to her."

He fell silent, embarrassed and fearful of reprimand.

"And who might this Sister be, who commands such devotion," the old lady mischievously enquired, enjoying his discomfiture, "who has such beauty that a man should walk so far just to see her face?"

"Mother, her name is Ida, and the journey I have undertaken is made easy at the thought of her coming. I beg you, do not refuse my request."

The wise old woman moved to the doorway she had come from, where waited one of the Sisters.

"Summon our good Sister Ida to come to me here," she said.

The nun bobbed a curtsy and disappeared into the convent.

"Take good care of her, my son," she said to the waiting John, "she is a good child and deserves far better than life has yet given her."

"With all my heart I promise I will care for her as no man before has cared for a woman," he replied, and she was content, as she looked into the earnest young face, that he told the truth. Knowing this made it easier for her to release the girl into his care.

They turned together as the door opened and the nun reappeared, alone.

"Good Mother, Sister Ida is not in her room. She was not at matins and did not break fast with us. No-one has seen her since dusk yesterday when they were returning from the city."

The old lady frowned, puzzled.

"Did she go out alone?" she asked.

"No, she went in a party of four, but Ida stayed a little after the others returned, at the house of an old woman near the wharf. Just for a few minutes, she said, but she has not yet returned."

* * * * *

They had chosen well, Ida's abductors. Tales of the ghost of a Roman legionnaire kept the superstitious souls of the city away from the old castle ruins. Ida's shouts for help had gone unheard, the baby's cries unnoticed. She lay in the darkness, very weak now, the loss of blood and the numbing cold of the cell bringing death ever closer.

The boy had died some hours earlier, she knew, but still she held him, rocked him, crooned a little song to him through broken, bloodied lips, gently stroked the tiny, unseen face. She told him about his father, how he was tall and handsome, and that soon, very soon now, he would come for them, take them away from this place, into the sunshine and the fresh, clean air, to walk the green fields near the sparkling river.

As above them, in the city streets, John and the nuns searched, Ida died, the child she had never seen clutched to her breast.

For a week they combed the city, John and the Sisters of St. Mary's, enlisting the monks of St. Werburgh's to help them. They retraced the route from the house where she had last been seen, back to the convent, but without success. Many people knew Ida, but none had seen her.

She had vanished without trace, and it quickly became apparent to all but John that their efforts were in vain. Yet, long after the others gave up, John searched on, his mind a turmoil of self-recrimination and grief. His distress was plain for all to see and the Mother Superior did all she could to comfort him, but he was beyond consolation.

While he suffered, Sister Ambrose rejoiced. Her revenge had been sweet, and the realisation that this man had been Ida's lover, and was suffering agonies of doubt, added further to her sadistic pleasure.

101

Rees had lain low while the search was on, now it was time for him to move on, back to his home across the Dee in Wales. As darkness fell he set out to cross the old stone bridge, in the pack on his back the gold and silver he had accumulated from the hideout in the forest and his criminal activities since his arrival in Chester. The pickings had been good, he thought, feeling the weight of the straps digging into his shoulders, good enough to set him up for life back in his native village. The final pay-off, from Sister Ambrose, had been the icing on the cake.

"Stupid bitch," he grinned to himself. "I enjoyed the job – I didn't need paying, it was a pleasure."

Out of the darkness, full into his face, came a yellow-eyed, pitch-black demon, spitting, hissing, scratching at his cheeks, driving him back against the parapet of the bridge where he overbalanced and fell the thirty or so feet into the river below. The shock as his body hit the water drove the breath from his lungs, the impact almost stunning him. Vainly, he tried to draw breath but succeeded only in swallowing water. He kicked and thrashed in an attempt to swim, his hands clawing at the water, his feet pushing vainly into the depths, seeking some foothold which wasn't there. The tide was in full ebb, the current strong, carrying him along like a broken stick, turning and tumbling in the force of its flow.

He struggled to release the pack which he had only minutes earlier strapped so very carefully and securely on to his back, the pack containing the sacks of gold and silver he had spent so long accumulating, the pack which was now killing him. A scream of frustration and terror choked in his throat as the weight dragged him to the bottom and drowned him.

Rees died a rich man.

Above him, on the parapet of the bridge, his attacker watched as the killer struggled, its wide yellow eyes fixed on his death throes. Then, when no sign of him remained, on silent paws, with a swish of its long, black tail, the cat disappeared into the darkness...

Chapter Twenty-Three

Finally, a weary and dispirited John was forced to concede that further searching was fruitless. Between them the search parties had exhausted every avenue of hope. Of Ida there was no trace, she had disappeared as if from the face of the earth. And so, on a rainy morning, he made his farewells to his fellow searchers and set out on the long, lonely journey back to Norton, hoping against hope that Ida might have gone there seeking him, that their paths had somehow crossed on the journey.

Late in the evening that hope, too, was dashed. He was warmly greeted by his brethren at the priory but no word had been received and of his lover there was no trace.

He did not give up hope immediately. The sisters of St. Mary's had promised to get word to him should Ida reappear in Chester, but, as the months dragged by without news, he was forced to accept that it was unlikely he would ever see her again. Her loss was a tremendous blow to him. For weeks he went about his duties automatically, lacking the will and enthusiasm he had previously shown. His conduct and bearing was brought to the notice of the Prior who called him to his office for some advice. John decided that the time had come to make a full confession of his involvement with Ida, and, as he did so, the kindly old Prior nodded his understanding and sympathy.

"God has given you this test, my son," he consoled John, "and, if it is His will, she will one day return to you. But now you must decide your future. This is a house of God, and only those who wish to serve Him may dwell here. Tomorrow I must have your decision. Will you dedicate the rest of your life to your Maker, or go from this place to seek earthly gratification?"

That night sleep evaded him. Throughout the long night he tossed and turned, his thoughts returning constantly to Ida, his memory taking him back to the brief time they had shared together, his mind full of guilt that he had betrayed her trust, broken his vow to her. The fault was not his, true, the delay had been unavoidable. Nevertheless he had failed her, and the guilt gnawed at his soul.

When morning came he had reached his decision. He would stay at the Priory, take his vows and his place amongst the monks of Norton. Two factors weighted his decision, firstly, that he felt in need of the comfort and support of his brothers there, and, more importantly, he would be where she expected him to be should she yet seek him out.

The future would prove that this was the correct decision to make, though many years would pass before his hopes were to be fulfilled, and, at the same time, shattered.

In Chester, too, there was one whose hopes went unfulfilled. Sister Ambrose had thought that, with Ida's passing, her life could return to what she considered to be normality. There were other younger nuns, weaker than Ida, on whom she had designs, and she had thought to recommence her lewd practices as soon as it was possible.

She had not reckoned on the cat.

She had first noticed it the day after Ida's entombment. That morning, as she crossed the courtyard, she spotted it crouching on a wall, its great yellow eyes following her progress, motionless except for the twitching of the tip of its tail.

Since then it had appeared everywhere she went, always silent, but the eyes saying everything, staring into her black soul, planting there the seeds of dread. Only when she approached it would it make a sound, spitting and growling then as it backed away from her, and always the unblinking, feral eyes, never leaving her face.

She knew fear now. She saw death in those eyes, as she had seen it in Ida's eyes on the day of Sister Catherine's funeral, and she knew, too, that she was not rid of Ida, would never be, so long as this creature lived.

Chapter Twenty-Four

As the months passed without news of his Ida, hope faded and John immersed himself deeper into his work and studies, gaining a degree of comfort from the faith he felt beginning to grow within him. His initial sense of bitterness had passed, to be replaced by a reluctant acceptance of the facts. Ida had gone, perhaps for good, and maybe he would not see her again, but never would he forget her, nor the love he felt for her. Now, that love could be dedicated to his present life and undertaking. She was his inspiration as he worked, in his dreams when he slept, in his prayers when he prayed; she would be a part of him forever, this he knew.

Her inspiration drove him on and, as time went by, his status at the Priory grew. The number of monks at Norton was very few, and soon he was regarded by the rest as one of the leaders. Within a year the Prior, in his eightieth year, passed peacefully away, after naming John as his successor. It was a decision accepted readily by his fellows, most of them too, being elderly and rather frail, ready to let a younger, stronger man take on the arduous responsibility of running the establishment.

While John flourished in this new status, a few miles away, in Chester, Sister Ambrose suffered ongoing torment.

The cat was with her constantly, by day and by night, stalking her, haunting her. She saw it when others did not, heard its hiss in the night, locked in her cell. Its eyes lit up her nightmares, more frequent now than ever, robbing her of sleep. Slowly, she was losing her sanity.

In her worldly wisdom, the old Abbess sensed trouble. Something was amiss, that much was apparent. She had suspected something of the affair between Sister Ambrose and Sister Martine, had known of such cases before, and could understand Ambrose's distress when Martine had died. Of Ida's part in the business she was not aware, but the death of Sister Catherine, she was sure, was also somehow tied in with it.

Then had come Ida's disappearance, the young monk's visit, seeking Ida. The lengthy but fruitless search for the girl had followed. Now there was Ambrose's strange behaviour and constant obsession with the presence of some strange cat which had arrived on the scene.

Although she had been a member of the Order for over sixty years and had unshakeable faith in God, the old woman still remembered the old gods and their worshippers and the chilling tales of witches and ghosts from her childhood days.

Something evil was happening, she sensed, something beyond her control. She must watch developments and try to be prepared for whatever should occur. In her prayers she asked God for His help.

In her terror-crazed mind Sister Ambrose was now convinced that Ida had escaped from her tomb. Since the night they had tortured and entombed Ida she had never been back to the scene, but now she felt compelled to go. The girl had barely been alive when they had left her, but could it be that she had survived? She must go to that awful place, check that the stone was still there, her victim still within. She wished now that her evil accomplice was here to help her, unaware that he had gone to a watery grave some months before.

Jumbled thoughts chased each other through her crazed mind: the girl was the cat, the cat was the Devil, therefore the girl was the Devil and was coming to take her. The girl had been a witch, she had used poisons and spells, killed Martine, should have been burned or drowned, that's why she was out, must burn her, that's how to kill a witch, burn her or drown her, stop her walking, close those eyes, stop them staring, burning into her soul...

Late that night, accompanied by two of her nuns, the Mother Superior followed Sister Ambrose as she left the convent. Her progress was erratic as every few yards she stopped, talking to herself, and, on one occasion, kicking out at some imaginary creature at her feet, a creature not visible to those following.

As they neared the old castle ruins one of the young nuns made the sign of the cross, fearful of the rumours of hauntings in the area and seeking Divine protection. The night was cold, a thin, sickle moon flitting between dark clouds providing the only light. They left the road and moved in amongst the ruins, watching as Sister Ambrose vanished down the short flight of steps leading to the deserted cellars, where she and her accomplice had so cruelly tormented the girl before leaving her imprisoned and, they presumed, dying.

From their vantage point above her they watched as she scrabbled at the pile of stones, tearing at them and casting them haphazardly aside until the huge stone slab was revealed. By this time Ambrose was babbling crazily to herself, snatches of the creed mingling with awful curses as she heaved at the stone, vainly trying to move it.

The nuns moved silently down the steps until they stood behind the gibbering figure of Ambrose. Then, in a wavering yet clear voice the old lady cried out: "What devil's work is this, Sister?".

Sister Ambrose shrieked in terror at the sound of the voice and tried to scramble away, tripping and tumbling as she went, then sobbing hysterically as she lay in the dirt. She babbled on and on, the words tripping over themselves in her rush to unburden her miserable soul in confession. The horror of what she was hearing shook the old nun. She shook her head in disbelief at what she was hearing, yet she immediately understood the awful truth.

"Bind her, and get her to her feet," she ordered her companions, her frail voice trembling with emotion. "We must get away from this place now. We shall return at daybreak."

They half carried, half dragged the hysterical woman up the steps and back to the convent, unresisting, seemingly resigned to her fate.

As they crossed the courtyard to the door they saw the black cat sitting in the doorway. It moved aside as they approached, then sat watching as they passed through and into the convent.

Sister Ambrose was locked into her cell and one of the young sisters posted as guard outside, even though she had made no attempt to resist or escape. Another of the nuns was sent to summon the sheriff, and, when he arrived, the Mother Superior told him of her suspicions and of what they had seen and heard, concluding by saying: "I fear we shall find our Sister Ida behind the stone. Tomorrow we shall see."

She was the first to enter the cellar the next morning as the slab was rolled away by the sheriff and his men, and the horror of the scene that the flickering light of her candle revealed was to live with her the rest of her life.

There was no smell of decay and she realised that, because of the conditions in the cell, low temperature and a supply of air, putrefaction had not begun to take place. Her heart pounded as she saw not one, but two bodies, one so tiny as to at first escape her notice. The bodies were partially mummified, the skin shrivelled and tight-drawn across the facial bones. Ida's once beautiful face was set in a rictal smile, the lips drawn back from shrunken gums and teeth which seemed too large for the mouth. The face of the baby was just a mass of wrinkled skin, its poor toothless little mouth open as if in supplication.

The anguish she felt at the sight of the two stone-blind pairs of eyes dully reflecting the flickering light, was greater than any she had ever felt before.

Now she understood, and the tears flowed down her cheeks as she tried to imagine the agonies this poor girl had endured before the moment of her dying. Through all her piety and gentleness there welled a flood of hatred so great that had Sister Ambrose been there at that moment, she would surely have killed her with her own hands.

She backed out of the hole and faced the sheriff and his men.

"She is there," she confirmed. "Go to the convent and remove the killer from our house. Roll back the stone and leave some men to watch over it until we return. She is one of our own and we shall take care of the arrangements here."

Back at St. Mary's she dispatched nuns to bring cerecloth and a casket for the remains while the men moved away to take Ambrose to gaol. Only she had seen the body of the baby and she now worked quickly to conceal it, wanting to save Ida from the revelation of her indiscretion, and, though less important, the

Order from scandal and shame. She went to the font where she knelt in prayer for a few moments, before filling a small phial with holy water.

The baby could not go unbaptised to its grave, innocent as it was of any sin. At the thought of the tiny body her eyes filled again with tears and her heart with loathing for the murderess locked away in the nearby castle gaol.

Returning to the scene of the heinous crime, the old lady instructed the sheriff's men to once again drag away the slab of stone.

"Give me a few moments alone with her," she said. "Come in when I call. She must be given the sacrament before she is moved."

To the accompanying Sisters she said: "Wait here and while you wait pray for her soul, that she might receive God's grace."

She entered the semi-darkness of the tomb, imagining once more the horrific circumstances and the terror in the total darkness as the young girl had died. She shuddered and wept again.

"Your secret shall be safe with me," she murmured.

"Come, my little one," she whispered to the shrivelled little body, taking it, not without considerable effort, from the arms of the tragic mother who had nursed it to the last. In its innocent nakedness it was revealed as a boy, a son who would never know his father, had never seen the face of his mother. Pity welled within her and she wrapped the little body in a piece of the cloth she had brought. Looking round the cell she observed a shelf-like recess cut into the rock wall and gently placed the pathetic little bundle on it, concealing it from view with a few pieces of stone from the floor.

"There shall be no shame for you, little man, and none for your mother – she deserves better than that."

She covered the body of Ida with the rest of the cloth and called for the others to come in. Gently the body was removed, wrapped in the cloth and placed in the casket, ready for its journey back to the convent. When they arrived there the Sisters carefully washed, as best they could, the hardened crusts of blackened blood from Ida's mummified corpse. They tended the tangled hair and ravaged face then dressed her in a clean new habit.

That night she was laid out in her casket before the altar in the Lady Chapel, and the Mother Superior gave instructions to prepare for her funeral the next morning.

As evening fell the old lady slipped quietly away from the convent carrying a wicker basket on her arm. Back at the tomb she removed the child's body from the shelf where she had hidden it and carried it, in the basket, down to the edge of the river.

In a simple little ceremony she baptised the child, naming him John, for her intuition told her that such was the name of his father. She then placed a couple of large stones in the basket with the body, bound the whole together with a length of twine and, using a broken branch she found nearby, pushed it well out into the stream. It floated a few yards downstream on the strong current before sinking gently below the surface.

For a few moments more she remained at the water's edge in prayer, then, with a deep sigh she climbed to her feet and, heavy-hearted, turned her wise old face towards heaven.

"Lord, forgive me my sin, and that of my sister, and take to Thy care this fruit of her sin, this I beseech Thee," she prayed.

* * * * *

Four tall, ornamental candlesticks stood around the casket in the chapel and the flickering light from them was reflected in the eyes of the large black cat as he sat motionless on the altar. All else was darkness.

Chapter Twenty-Five

The day had dawned bright and sunny, as befitted the occasion, and the sunlight had illuminated the little church, streaming through the stained-glass windows, casting the intense brilliance of their colours into the otherwise gloomy interior. One beam, in particular, had seemed to stretch from the scene at the font right back to the window from whence it came, a soft golden path of light leading towards the heavens beyond the glass. For a moment, Ian's mind wandered from what was going on, and the words on the gravestone, since the birth largely forgotten, suddenly and clearly came back to him:

"THE SOULS OF THOSE THAT DIE
ARE BUT SUNBEAMS LIFTED HIGHER."

The voice of the young priest brought him back to the present and the service being enacted.

"Peter John, I baptise thee in the Name of the Father, and of the Son, and of the Holy Ghost, Amen."

The child had slept through the service so far, but the wetting of his head, discreet as it had been, was sufficient to rouse him and Peter John gave vent to his displeasure in the way of babies the world over. He filled his little lungs and yelled.

All that had been several hours before, at the little church in the nearby picture-postcard village of Whitegate. Now, with friends and family departed and the debris of the party cleared away, Jane and Ian reflected on the day. Peter John slept soundly on the settee between them, exhausted by his big day, his cherubic face showing no signs of the tantrums of earlier.

"What a little devil," said Ian. "Just look at him now – butter wouldn't melt in his mouth."

Jane laughed. "Did you see your mother's face in the church when he was screaming and squirming? She was so embarrassed at the noise."

"Well, she's not heard him at full pitch before, she's only seen his quiet side until today."

111

It was true. On the few occasions they had received visitors since the birth, the young man had displayed impeccable manners, sleeping between his feeds, making up for the hours at night when sleep was denied them all. Ian and Jane were exhausted, and, with teething soon to come, not hopeful that things would greatly improve in the immediate future. However, they were well into spring now and the promise of better weather gave their spirits a boost.

This would be their first full summer together, as a family, in the house, and they talked contentedly now of all the things they could do together, the walks through the woods, bird-watching, picnics, all the things they had not done because of the feud they had carried on for the past six months or so.

Well – that was all behind them now and things were going to be different...

Chapter Twenty-Six

That night, in the dungeons beneath the castle, Sister Ambrose was introduced to Hell. In the semi-darkness of her cell, lit only by the intermittent, guttering light of the rush torch fixed to the wall of the passage outside, she saw devils.

They came for her with their blood-red eyes and gaping mouths, flashing white fangs and great hooked claws slashing at her arms and face. Time and again she hit out at them, screaming in terror at their approach, frustrated at her failure to make contact with them. But hit them she could not, for they were the devils of her mind, whirling and swooping round her head, mocking her attempts to catch them.

Then, gradually, the various figures merged into one, this a gigantic ebony cat, big as a goat, huge yellow eyes staring into hers, drilling into her deranged mind. It crept nearer as she cowered against the wall of the cell, stalking her as she babbled incoherently in her madness. Great jaws gaped open, saliva dripping from glistening ivory incisors as long as carving knives as they reached for her throat.

Then, mercifully, the dreadful creature was gone, and in its place stood Ida. The yellow eyes were replaced by startling blue, the feline snarl by gentle smile, and entreating arms were outstretched towards Ambrose, drawing her into an embrace she was unable to resist, hugging her to her breast, as though in forgiveness and comfort.

Sister Ambrose knew that this was not possible: Ida was dead... Yet the pain that stabbed through her chest as the arms tightened round her like a vice was very real, squeezing the breath from her lungs, rupturing her evil heart and driving all traces of life from her miserable, bedevilled frame.

At the same time as the gaoler discovered her body the next morning, less than half a mile away, at the convent of St. Mary, that of Ida was being laid to rest.

In a simple yet moving service she was endowed with the full rights of a practising nun of the Order, even though she had not taken her final vows, and her body was then laid to rest, with due ceremony, in the crypt beneath the convent, the third to be so interred there in a very short space of time. Though none was aware of the fact, she was two months short of her eighteenth birthday.

Chapter Twenty-Seven

S ome years had passed since Ida's murder but the Mother Superior was still much troubled. Her conscience nagged at her, telling her to confide in someone else the secret that she alone held.

At the priory of Norton, John's rise to prominence continued. As Prior, he was now in line for further advancement, and just such an opportunity had arisen with the death of the Abbot of St. Mary's at Vale Royal. John was an obvious candidate as his successor. He was young, strong, and, since the loss of Ida, which he had finally and reluctantly accepted as fact, totally dedicated to his faith and the Order. All the love he had felt for her, he had transferred to his work, and his reward was now to be endowed with the abbacy of the place where that love had been both born and requited.

News of his appointment filtered through the countryside and within the Order there was general approval. John had become a popular figure as Prior of Norton and would be sadly missed there, but none begrudged him the honour. With the appointment, as was common practice, came a change of name and John of Dutton, Prior of Norton, became Peter, fifth Abbot of the Monastery of St. Mary at Vale Royal.

When the news reached St. Mary's convent in Chester the Mother Superior's dilemma was solved. It was apparent to her that God was directing her actions. In guiding Ida's lover, and the father of her child, back to the place where she knew they had met, He was telling her what she must do. She must go to Peter, make him cognisant of the facts, give him the opportunity to put matters to rights.

Arrangements were quickly made and, two days later, she arrived at Vale Royal. The lessons of the previous journey had been well learned and this time she had travelled with a strong, armed escort and the trip had been smooth and uneventful. She was warmly received by Abbot Peter, who she still thought of as

John, and given refreshment after her tiring journey. Later, in his private chamber she had begun her story.

"Lord Abbot, forgive me, but I bring sad tidings. A long time now I have been burdened with the knowledge which I must ask your forbearance in revealing."

Looking into the troubled old face, Peter knew what he was about to hear and nodded.

"You were always the wise one, good Mother. It saddens me to have caused you such pain. Pray unburden your soul, that I might share your sorrow."

Slowly, hesitantly, the old lady related the sad story, omitting nothing. As she told of that dreadful day they had found Ida and her baby the tears ran down the wrinkled face in streams.

Strangely, Peter was the stronger of the two. He comforted the woman in her distress, thanked her for her efforts in protecting his and Ida's names and the Order from disgrace. He knew what a strain she must have been living under since the awful event, living a lie, keeping her dreadful secret.

As the words flowed he felt a deep sadness, a great pain, that he would never again see the beautiful face of his beloved Ida, hear her laughter, feel her body against his. He mourned too, the loss of the son he would never see, a son conceived here, in these idyllic surroundings which were now his domain.

The old lady finished her story and sat, head bowed, before him. He reached out and placed a hand on her shoulder. She looked up and, in his face, saw the pain she was feeling mirrored there. After a while he spoke.

"I made a vow to my Ida that one day we would be together again in this place. Though she is dead, I must yet fulfil that vow. Good Mother, with your blessing I will bring her here, that her wish may be granted. In life I have failed her, help me to comfort her spirit in death."

In that moment the old lady saw him, not as a mighty Abbot, but as the ordinary man he was, asking for her help, mourning his lost love. She, in turn, reached out to him and he fell to his knees before her, begging for forgiveness. She drew him to his feet.

"For my part, there is nothing to forgive; for your sins against God you must ask His pardon. I know you loved her truly. I will help you in what you ask. You shall bring her to her last resting place here."

The following day they made the return journey to Chester and, late that evening, Peter experienced the greatest pain of his life as he gazed down on the poor face he had loved. The nuns had done their best when laying out the body to remove the ravages which death had brought, the oils and salves they had used creating an impression of repose. Gone was the smile, true, and the blue eyes were closed for ever, yet still, to his eyes, there was a basic beauty that death could not destroy. He bent and kissed the cold, dead lips.

"Come home, my darling," he whispered.

All night he sat beside the casket in the crypt, watching over her, slipping into and out of sleep. A single candle cast a flickering light around the crypt, reflected from the far shadows by the yellow eyes of another watcher.

Next morning the casket was sealed again, removed from the crypt and loaded onto a cart ready for its last journey. Peter made his farewells and the cart moved slowly away. As it passed beneath the archway leaving the courtyard, the cat dropped silently into it and nestled contentedly against the coffin. As they passed alongside the river Peter searched the surface, wondering at what point the body of his child had slipped beneath the water. As he searched the tears flowed freely down his cheeks.

The remainder of the journey was uneventful and Peter sat quietly on the cart, engrossed in his own thoughts. The mood was broken when they came to the spot where the ambush had taken place, where he had first met the brave young woman who had saved his life and stolen his heart.

He ordered the driver to halt the cart and dismounted. For a few moments he knelt in prayer beneath the tree where she had made her stand against the robbers, seeing in his mind's eye the flashing eyes and heaving breast as she fought them off. Through his sorrow he smiled, a lump in his throat at the memory. He rose to his feet and remounted the cart.

"Drive on," he ordered, "we shall take her home."

Chapter Twenty-Eight

It had been one of the warmest summers for years. Day after day the sun had shone and Jane revelled in its warmth. Each morning she walked, with her son, the paths through the woods and around the golf course. One such path led through an area known as the Lady Wood, within which was situated a small lake called Rookery Pool. On this morning this was the path she had chosen. They were later than usual and, as they passed through the wood, in the clearings, out of the shade, the sun's rays were fierce.

"It's a scorcher today, isn't it?" she remarked to young Peter as he bounced happily in his pushchair. " We mustn't keep you out too long today or you'll burn."

His only answer was an agitated wave of a chubby arm and a loud squeal which set off a raucous chorus, amongst the treetops, from the birds which had given the pool its name.

She stopped in a shady spot overlooking the water and unstrapped the child, setting him free from his mobile prison. In a flash he tried to get away, crawling unsteadily towards the water and a man fishing there. Jane followed him indulgently and caught him in her arms before he reached the angler. The sound of their approach had disturbed the man and he turned, smiling as he saw the struggling child trying to escape his mother's clutches.

"You've got your hands full there, love," he smiled.

"You're not joking," Jane replied. "I'm sorry if we've disturbed you."

"No problem," he said. "I've been here since dawn and the bites have dried up now. I was just thinking of packing up, anyway."

He was a man of about fifty or so, fair hair turning to grey. His twinkling bright blue eyes smiled at her from a suntanned face, a curly pipe hung from his jaw and she caught the aromatic smell of his tobacco. She felt herself blushing beneath his gaze and taking a firmer grip on Peter she turned away.

"Bye-bye, Sunshine," she heard him call, and looking back saw him wave a casual hand at the boy, who replied with a huge smile of his own and a delighted wave.

Reaching the spot where they had left the pushchair she stood for a few moments more, watching the angler, his back to her now, as he settled easily into his obviously well-practiced and contented routine. Then, plonking the protesting boy back into his chair and strapping him in, she turned for home. She followed the path through the wood, happy to be in the dappled shade of the trees, till they reached the drive leading across the front of the clubhouse and down to the house.

Back in the cool of the kitchen she prepared some food and a drink, for herself and the boy, then settled into her afternoon routine. She changed from her walking clothes into shorts and bikini top, and, taking their lunch with her, went onto the lawn at the rear of the house.

After checking that the garden gates were locked so that Peter could not wander, she first fed the youngster then consumed her own meal.

As she ate she watched lovingly as Peter crawled around the garden. His energy and curiosity seemed boundless. Each bed of flowers was carefully examined, with a few blooms being removed rather abruptly, until her words and tone of voice caused him to stop. The rockery became a miniature mountain range to be scaled, the lawn a sports field as he determined to cross it, little arms and legs pumping him along until the inevitable collapse and yell of anguish.

After the third such tumble she carried him into the shade of the parasol and gave him a drink. He was tired now after his exertions and as she held him she rocked him gently. In only a few minutes his eyes closed and he fell asleep.

For a little while she sat holding him where he lay, gazing down at the flushed, cherubic face with a love she could not have explained to anyone. Then she rose from her chair and transferred him to a rug laid on the grass in the shade of a large parasol.

"That's enough sun for you today, my little treasure," she

whispered, "any more and you'll be sore and grumpy."

Having seen to the boy's requirements she stretched out on the sun-lounger, luxuriating in the warmth of the sun's rays. She gazed down the length of her body as she lay there. Her tan was almost all-over by now and she had got her figure back very well after Peter's birth – a fact which had not gone unnoticed by Ian.

She smiled as she thought of her husband, a slow, delicious smile which spread across her lovely face. She glanced at her watch. Only three hours till he would be home.

"Hope he won't be too tired," she mused. "I'll just have to make sure he's not."

The effects of the meal, her morning walk and the heat of the afternoon combined to bring on a heavy drowsiness and a few moments later she fell into a deep sleep, her thoughts on her husband's homecoming and the welcome she would give him...

Chapter Twenty-Nine

During the remainder of the journey Peter's thoughts were concentrated on the question of his Ida's last resting place and by the time they reached the tree-lined drive leading to the Abbey his mind was made up.

She would, he had decided, have a place of honour normally reserved only for incumbent Abbots at their time of death, namely, in the crypt beneath the great High Altar within the Abbey itself. As the cart entered the main gate of the establishment he called to one of the attendant monks.

"Go find the master mason. Send him to me – I have important work for him."

At the sound of his voice the cat stirred, leapt gracefully down from the cart and disappeared, unseen, into the nearby garden.

Ida's coffin was taken from the cart into the Lady Chapel, there to await its move to its final destination, and once more Peter spent a few moments in prayer kneeling beside it. He concluded by addressing the casket,

"That pledge I made to bring us together again in this place I now fulfil. My heart is aching that you cannot see me, cannot hear me. May God grant you the knowledge."

When the mason arrived Peter laid out his requirements. In the crypt, deep beneath the High Altar the craftsman was to construct a special burial chamber. It was to be large enough to contain two stone sarcophagi, he explained, for it was his intent to be laid alongside Ida on his death. They would be the best that money could buy, hewn from local stone, as were the stones of the Abbey, by the finest masons in the district.

Directly above the chamber, in front of the Altar, there was to be erected a gravestone, a monument to Ida's memory which would stand for all time. The mason was to produce drawings for him to choose the most suitable design, and all was to be ready as quickly as possible. Too long already had Ida suffered great indignity, now she was to be honoured as she deserved.

Work commenced apace. Wagons were despatched to the quarry at Eddesbury to bring stone for the tasks he had set. Two great blocks were chosen for the coffins and the masons set to carving them out. Others worked in the crypt, building the burial chamber, whilst a third group was given the task of carving the stones for the monument Peter had chosen as Ida's memorial.

He had changed the mason's plans only slightly. During his time at the convent in Chester he had noticed, in the grounds there, an elaborately carved artifact which he now thought it would be fitting to incorporate into Ida's monument. To this end he had despatched two of his men with a letter to the Mother Superior, requesting that he might be given her permission to use it so, thus establishing for all time a link with her tragically short life there.

By the end of the month all the work was complete. The monument was erected in front of the High Altar, a splendid work in rich, red sandstone, topped with the headpiece he had received from Chester.

As he stood before it on the day of its completion, a ray of sunlight shone directly onto it through the coloured glass of one of the chevet windows, like a golden staircase leading the eye, and the soul perhaps, to Heaven.

At that moment came unbidden into his mind these words:
"The souls of those that die are but sunbeams lifted higher."
He turned to the mason and repeated the words.

"The souls of those that die are but sunbeams lifted higher. Carve these words well, my friend, they shall be her epitaph."

Next day the body of Ida was laid to rest in the chamber beneath the altar, with next to her the empty casket, waiting for the time when her lover should join her.

* * * * *

The wait was not to be a long one. Two years later, on a punitive raid against Welsh bandits near the border, Peter and a party of his men were ambushed and he and another monk were murdered.

The killers escaped and took refuge in Holt Castle, on the River Dee. Peter's body was returned to his beloved Vale Royal and laid to rest alongside that of Ida, as had been his request.

Decreed by fate to spend but a short time together in life, they now faced eternity together, re-united in death.

Chapter Thirty

During one of her afternoon walks Jane had sought out the site of the Nun's Grave. Since Peter's birth Ian had hardly mentioned the subject, the youngster now occupying all his spare time, taking his mind off his research, for which Jane was extremely grateful. His interest in this monument and the story behind it had been in danger of becoming an obsession, a morbid preoccupation she had not cared for, but something which, she had now decided, she needed to understand for herself. She had never before visited the site, but knew well enough where it was from Ian's previous talk of it, and it took only a few minutes for her to reach the spot.

As she looked at the edifice she felt a shiver of apprehension run through her. There was something evil here, she thought. Something which had nearly broken up her marriage, taken from her the only man she had ever loved. Instinctively, she knew the threat was still there and again she shuddered.

Abruptly, she turned the pushchair and hurried away. As she did so she imagined she heard the sound of music, muffled and far away, and another noise, a cry, no, more like a sigh, long, drawn-out, a lonely, heart-rending sound, like nothing she had ever heard. Scared now, she glanced around, but saw nothing to account for the noises. She hurried on.

From its resting place in the grass nearby, the big black cat rose and stretched, then followed silently the path she had taken.

Once more her route led her to the Rookery Pool and there, in the same spot, sat the angler she had seen before. Alerted again by the sound of their approach, Peter's joyful yells stirring all around him, the man turned and smiled.

"I thought I recognised that voice," he said. "How is my little sunshine today?"

From his pocket he drew his battered old pipe and a box of matches. Within seconds he was puffing contentedly at it and the smell of the tobacco smoke brought to Jane a sudden memory of her grandfather, whom she had known for only a few years before he died.

The angler's air of tranquillity and contentment calmed Jane and she felt rather foolish at her fear of a few moments before. She felt safe and comfortable with this gentle man and suddenly she felt she needed to talk.

"Why do you call him 'Sunshine'?" she asked the man. "His name is Peter John Barker. Say 'hello', Peter."

The boy responded with another piercing squeal and the angler grinned again.

"Pleased to meet you, too," he replied. "My name's Alan."

"And I'm Jane. We live in one of the new houses over there."

She waved a hand vaguely in the direction of home.

"Very nice, too," said Alan. "Do you like it round here?"

She felt so at ease with this man that once the conversation started it just seemed to flow.

As they talked she became aware of his love of nature in general, and of this area in particular. He told her he had lived in the district all his life and his great pride and interest in its history became obvious to her as they talked further.

They talked of many things, of birds and flowers, trees and water, until, eventually she manoeuvred him around to the subject she really wanted to ask him about.

"Can you tell me anything about the Nun's Grave near the big house?" she asked.

She saw the change in his expression, the smile was gone, a sudden wariness in his eyes. In an instant the mood had changed, the bond was broken. Taking the old pipe from his mouth he turned almost rudely back to his tackle and, his back towards her now, he growled:

"Leave it alone. Keep away from it, it's private. Just forget all about it. No good can come from meddling with such things. Keep away, and keep that little boy away, too."

She sat a while longer, Peter dozing in the warm sunshine at her side, but Alan made no further attempts to talk to her. Her mention of the Nun's Grave had, it seemed, killed the conversation stone dead. She rose to her feet and picked the boy up, moving slowly away towards the pushchair. He remained with his back toward her, rod in hand, not even turning as they left.

"Goodbye, then," she ventured. "See you again soon?"

His only reply was a surly, noncommittal grunt.

She was puzzled and annoyed at his sudden change of mood, brought about, she realised by her query about the Nun's Grave.

"I knew there was something about that place," she mused. "It had got to Ian, taken him over. Now here's another man it's affected. It's as if they are bewitched or something. They ought to knock the damned thing down – get rid of it altogether."

Peter John gurgled his agreement and struggled to escape his harness. The sound and movement broke the spell and she smiled.

"Come along my little treasure, it's time for some serious sunbathing for me and an afternoon nap for you."

Behind her she left a troubled man. Although he had never seen anything himself, Alan knew of others who swore there was a "presence" in the area of the old Manor House. One or two friends, members of the angling fraternity, had seen or heard things they couldn't explain, and he knew of a local historian who was compiling a record of such incidents and "sightings", the numbers of which were far too numerous to be scoffed at.

For the first time in nearly an hour his float slid beneath the surface and he struck, instinctively, his thoughts still on the girl. The fish was only small and he swung it towards him, reaching to catch it with his free hand. He misjudged slightly and caught the line just above the fish. The slackening of the line was all that the fish needed to shake the tiny, barbless hook free and it fell to the grass at his side where it lay, tail flipping in its efforts to regain the safety of the water. He put down the rod and rose from his seat to rescue the fish.

From the long grass nearby shot the figure of a large black cat. It snatched up the fish in its mouth then turned and ran. A few yards away it stopped and turned to face him once more. It dropped the still quivering fish to the grass and licked its chops, the yellow eyes holding his, glaring a challenge, daring him to come any closer.

He stopped, uncertain for a second, a ridiculous feeling of fear coming over him. The cat picked up the fish again and bit into it, crunching through scales and flesh into the still quivering body. All the while it ate, its eyes never left Alan's face. The moment of fear passed and the angler angrily stamped a booted foot. In a flash, the cat whirled away into the undergrowth and was gone, the only trace of its presence a few silver scales sparkling in the sunshine.

* * * * *

For the past two weeks the weather had been superb, and Jane's tan had deepened with each passing day. She had always been a sun-worshipper, enjoying nothing more than soaking up its rays in the privacy of her garden.

Each day, weather permitting, she would go through the same routine: a change of clothing for herself and the boy, set the answer-phone, prepare a light lunch, and out to the garden.

Today was to be one such day and, her routine complete, she locked the gate so that the toddler could not escape, before relaxing on the well-used sun-lounger. The morning walk, her meal and the heat of the day combined to send her quickly into a shallow sleep...

* * * * *

In her dream she was a nun. She walked slowly down a long avenue between majestic tall trees and into view came a magnificent, huge cathedral, resplendent in the evening sunshine. It had a massive square tower, ornately decorated with columns and statues of the saints. The coloured glass in its arched windows caught the sun's rays, reflected them in flashes of red, blue and green, giving the building the appearance of some great crown, set with precious jewels.

Her legs carried her, unbidden, through a stone portico and into the nave. The building was enormous, and as magnificent inside as out.

She floated slowly down the centre aisle, a bride of Christ, though dressed not in white but grey, and with her toddler son at her side. Her thoughts were both confused and confusing. Looking ahead she saw the figure of a monk, kneeling in prayer before the High Altar. As she approached he came to his feet and turned. She laughed. It was the fisherman, Alan, and he must be playing a joke on her. But he reached out his arms to her and said:

"Come, my love, see the place I have prepared for us."

He led her a few steps to one side and she was facing the old nun's grave in the garden near the golf club. But this time it was inside the building and it wasn't old, it was newly carved and a sunbeam lit up the name carved upon it, *Ida Marion Godman*...

Further words followed but she did not read them. She was Jane Barker, she was certain, yet she recognised and welcomed the love in the monk's words and she somehow understood that the grave was hers. She looked round for Peter John who had been playing in the grass behind the fisherman, but he had vanished...

* * * * *

She awoke with a shudder. The sun had dipped behind the trees, meaning that it was fairly late, and the afternoon had cooled considerably. Rubbing the sleep from her face she called to Peter, her eyes searching the garden for him as she did so. She heard the sound of his laughter beyond the garden fence, out of sight, and ran towards it, calling again, a strange, unreasoning terror now in her heart. She scrabbled up the fence and, as she clung to the top, was just in time to see a figure in a long grey cloak disappearing into the wood, the toddler in her arms chattering merrily away as they went.

Jane fell, rather than climbed, over the fence, landing heavily on the other side, knocking the breath from her body. She staggered to her feet and took off in pursuit of this woman who had dared to steal her baby. Murder was in her heart, a red mist of hatred for this bitch who had taken her Peter. She would kill her, scratch her bloody eyes out...

She fell again, tearing her face on a branch. Her near-naked body was scratched in a dozen places, her bare feet torn by the rough ground, but she staggered to her feet and ran on, following the sound of her baby's voice in the trees ahead, calling his name as she ran.

The trees thinned out and she found herself approaching the clearing near the old boat-house, a spot she had passed before. From there the path led upstream, towards the weir where the old mill had stood and, as she ran, she became aware of the thundering noise of the water as it fell over the sill of the weir into the foaming pool twenty feet below.

She reached the pool and saw the woman, standing, her back to Jane, on the high stone wall overlooking the water as it boiled and churned beneath her feet, baby Peter clutched to her breast. It was only then that Jane realised the significance of the clothes this woman was wearing.

"A nun, a bloody nun!" she screamed, now in a kind of madness, mouthing totally uncharacteristic obscenities. "I know you, you bitch, you're dead, you're bloody dead, you can't take my baby, I'll bloody kill you, you lousy bitch. Give me my baby, put my baby down, put him down..."

All the time she scrabbled nearer, the breath rasping harshly in her throat, hot tears streaming down her face and still the grey-clad figure had not moved.

Summoning up the last of her strength Jane reached the woman, grabbed her and spun her round, one hand striking out at her and the other snatching at the baby, crushing him to her breast.

There was no resistance from the other woman as Jane attacked her, sobbing hysterically, screaming foul profanities as she tore at the face. The face. There was something about the face: she had seen it before, but in her madness could not think straight. She knew that face, she had seen it before, but where?

She overbalanced and fell, still grasping her precious bundle, into the tossing foam below. Just before she drowned she caught one more glimpse of the nun, looking down on her, and she remembered where she had seen the face. It had smiled back at her from the bathroom mirror that very morning...

* * * * *

As he drove along the drive towards home Ian was hoping that she would still be wearing the yellow bikini, which showed off so well her golden tan, waiting for him to arrive home. She loved the sunshine and it had been another gorgeous day. He knew she would have been sunbathing, and he pictured her beautiful figure, waiting, just for him.

Instead, there were two police cars outside the house and Ian listened unbelievingly as one of the officers broke the news to him. His wife had apparently fallen into the river and drowned. Perhaps he could answer a few questions. Was she in the habit of walking the river banks alone? Had he known her to swim in the river?

Ian shook his head, unable to fully comprehend the awfulness of what he was hearing, stunned by the shock.

"She walked most days, with Peter, and she didn't swim very well. There's no way she would have gone in the river and left Peter on his own."

At this second mention of the boy's name the police officer stopped him.

"You mentioned Peter, sir, who is Peter?"

"He is my son. Where is he, is he all right?"

The puzzled expression on the officer's face gave him his answer and he groaned in agony at the realisation that the boy, too was missing.

"I'm sorry, sir, we didn't know there was anyone else involved."

It had been an angler who had spotted Jane's body drifting slowly downstream, some two hundred yards below the weirpool. He had run to the nearby lock-keeper's cottage and a phone call had set the wheels in motion. The body was swiftly recovered and enquiries round the nearby estate and golf club had helped the

131

police to pinpoint where Jane lived. All that it was necessary to do then was wait until Ian arrived home to break the tragic news to him.

The revelation that his son was also missing added to the tragedy. The police frogmen were called to the scene and an intensive search of the river, from the point where Jane's body had been discovered right back upstream to the weirpool, was carried out, without success.

Further exhaustive searches were made over the following days, covering the whole length of the Old River down to its junction with the main watercourse a mile or so downstream.

The body of the baby was never recovered.

Chapter Thirty-One

𝕴 hadn't fished the Old River for quite a long time, but I was pleased I'd come today. The shoals of roach aren't there like they used to be, but a few decent tench from the stretch below the weirpool had made the evening worthwhile. Only trouble is, it's such a long walk back to the car park, and I'm not getting any younger.

I packed my tackle into the car, lit my pipe and climbed wearily in. In the gathering gloom, I drove slowly through the arched vaults of trees along the drive towards its junction with the dual carriageway, my thoughts now drifting towards a couple of pints in the Bull's Head at Davenham.

I heard a sound from the rear seat and, glancing in the mirror, saw two faces looking back at me, a little toddler, laughing and pointing, and an old, old woman, with the oldest, darkest face I had ever seen.

The old face smiled, a smile lit up by a late sunbeam filtering through the trees, a smile fascinating in its antiquity, the eyes as black and dead as the pit...

Extract from the Northwich Clarion, 25 August 1997:-

"Northwich Police are appealing for witnesses following an horrific accident on Vale Royal Drive last Saturday, when a car ran off the road out of control, crashed into a tree and burst into flames.

"The occupant, a well-known local angler, perished in the fire.

"The police are particularly keen to interview a woman, vaguely described as wearing a long grey coat and carrying some sort of bundle, seen walking away from the scene of the accident.

"This is the second tragedy to strike the area recently, following closely on the drowning of a young mother and her baby in the river nearby."

THE END...?

Select Bibliography

Many books and documents were studied during the years when I researched the background for this novel and I would particularly like to thank the staff at Northwich's Brunner Library for their help and patience.

The major works which helped with my studies included:

Cheshire - Coward
Vale Royal Abbey and House - Winsford Local Historical Society, F H Thompson
Vale Royal Abbey - A thesis by H Jukes (1980)
Ida or the Mystery of the Nun's Grave at Vale Royal in Cheshire - J H Cooke
A manuscript by the Honorable Essex Cholmondeley (19th century)

Alan K Leicester

An imprint of
**ANNE LOADER
PUBLICATIONS**

Other books published by the Léonie Press, an imprint of
Anne Loader Publications, 13 Vale Road, Hartford, Northwich,
Cheshire CW8 1PL, Gt Britain, include:

Memories of a Cheshire Childhood by Lenna Bickerton
(ISBN 1 901253 00 7), price £4.99

A House with Sprit: A dedication to Marbury Hall by Jackie Hamlett
and Christine Hamlett (ISBN 1 901253 01 5), price £8.99

Kathleen: Memories of a girl who grew up in wartime
by K M Thomas (ISBN 1 901253 02 3), price £4.99

Ulu Tiram: A cameo of life in Malaya at the time of 'The Emergency'
by Peter Thomas and Kathleen Thomas (ISBN 1 901253 05 8),
price £5.75

*A Bull by the Back Door: How an English family find their own
paradise in rural France* by Anne Loader
(ISBN 1 901253 06 6), price £8.99

*The Way We Were: Omnibus edition of Les Cooper's Crewe memories
'Over My Shoulder' and 'Another's War'*
by Les Cooper (ISBN 1 901253 07 4), price £7.99

The Duck with a Dirty Laugh: More family adventures in rural France
by Anne Loader (ISBN 1 901253 09 0),
price £8.99